The First and Last Man on Earth

Robert J Walker

First published in 2023 by Blossom Spring Publishing
The First and Last Man On Earth © 2023
Robert J Walker ISBN 978-1-7393514-8-9
E: admin@blossomspringpublishing.com W:
www.blossomspringpublishing.com

Chapter 1

Troubled Times

Adam breathed in the calm as he strolled down the deserted street. Three days ago he had fought through the same route, carrying as much food as he could muster as crowds of frantic and scared Londoners prepared for the inevitable. War was coming.

Adam had failed miserably in his first war mission to procure some toilet roll. What irritated him immensely was that he was experienced in the art of hunting down the paper gold from his Covid days and yet, a few years later, his gathering skills seemed to have deserted him entirely. He hoped the war would wait because stocks were getting desperately low and he had no doubt that his lily-livered son would wet himself at the first sight of an Eastern Forces soldier charging at him down Park Lane.

Adam groaned. "Son," he said out loud to himself. "Son, daughter, nonbinary pain in the arse. I don't even know what to call him, her… it."

Adam groaned again. The Well Watered Garden, his favourite watering hole, was closed and had chipboard screwed across the decorative windows and door. A small gap in the wood revealed a painted snake's tail on the glass and he stared past as best he could with his face pressed against the sharp edge of the splintered board.

The Garden was dark and deserted like everywhere else. London, where possible, had moved underground. He noticed 'No war' was scrawled on every board in blue and red spray paint that was remarkably artistic.

'Agreed,' thought Adam to the sentiment. He trudged home empty handed.

Four hundred yards from his front door, Adam passed

the corner shop. Empty and deserted for days he was not expecting to find anything but, to his surprise, a pile of yesterday's newspapers was bundled and strapped in yellow bands as if ready for collection at the front door.

Adam looked around. There was no one around. He knocked at the shop door. No reply. He knocked again and shouted, "Hello. I'm taking the papers." No answer. "I hope it's ok. Sorry if it's not," he whispered under his breath.

He picked up the bundle and headed home. It was an awkward shape and tried hard to get between his knees to trip him up and if he hadn't been so close to home, he would have abandoned it.

Through a picket fence gate to the Victorian front door of his ridiculously expensive Victorian terraced house, paid for by the insurance money from the tragic loss of his wife, he paused and waited for the expected call.

"Adam," it came, as the door next to his opened to reveal the voice's owner. Standing in the entrance next door was a beautiful woman. She had long blonde hair, long eyelashes, long legs and she smiled longingly at him. Like she always did.

"Hi." He shyly grinned. "Want a copy of yesterday's news?" Adam nodded in the direction of his newspaper haul.

"No thanks." She beamed, with her smile sending butterflies sweeping through his body. "But I do have something for you."

She leaned inside and then reappeared and instantly threw a toilet roll in his direction. He caught it, dropping his newspapers in the process.

The toilet roll was wrapped in what looked like greaseproof paper and printed on the side in bottle green ink was 'Izal Medicated Toilet Paper'. Adam laughed out loud.

"This is that horrible school tracing paper stuff isn't it? Where on Earth did you get that from?"

"Oh well that's charming." The woman fake-frowned. "I find the one thing that half the country is looking for and you call it horrible." She pretended to wipe imaginary tears from her eyes, but her delicious smile gave away her true feelings.

"Oh don't cry, sweetheart." Adam played along. "I love you for getting me this. It will be only marginally harsher than the newspapers I was going to use. Seriously I'm super grateful. You're my hero. Where did you find it? I've looked everywhere. Where did you find it? Where was it?"

She was lost in her own thoughts. He had called her sweetheart but better still had said he loved her. Loved her. Adam said he loved her. She loved Adam. With all her heart. She had loved him for years. He had a broken heart, she knew that. He was always amazing towards her, she knew that. He had never shown an interest though and she knew that too. But now he loved her. That was all that mattered to her right now. Typical that as this monumental breakthrough occurred, war would unquestionably tear them apart.

"Helloooo. Anyone in there?" said Adam who she suddenly realised was staring at her looking somewhat bewildered.

"Sorry," she chuckled. "I have a lot on my mind at the moment."

"War or your Gran or both?" he asked. 'Neither – You!' she thought. "Both," she said.

"How's she doing?" said Adam, knowing the answer would not be good.

"Hours. Days. No longer. It can't come soon enough to be honest. She's in pain but barely conscious. She needs to go before the Commies come because I can't move her."

"Not really Commies," was perhaps the worst attempt at a terribly insensitive reply Adam could have mustered but her gorgeous smile and reply of "I know but no one really even knows who we're even fighting against so I went old school" made him feel like he got away with it.

"The toilet roll," he asked holding it aloft. "Where from?"

"My grandad bought about three million boxes of the stuff in the 1970s," she explained. "My grandmother has been using it ever since. Last few rolls now and I'd better go and check on her," she said as she turned with sad eyes to head inside.

"Take care, lovely," he shouted after her and her heart melted as she closed the door.

Adam smiled to himself, picked up his newspaper haul and headed inside through his forever-unlocked front door due to the catch being superglued open by his wife after their fourth time of being locked out. She irresponsibly never considered that they would then promptly lose all the keys for the main lock.

"Darren," he called to no reply as he wandered into the hall. "Darren. Darren. Darren where are you?"

There was no reply and Adam started to panic. There had been kidnappings and shanghaies as Guerrilla armies became established and Darren was a sitting duck. There was no way he would defend himself as a pacifist to a fault.

At school some chubby, spotty loser had stolen everything from his dinner money to his trainers from him and he had simply stood there and allowed it. Darren could have battered his bully any time he wanted to but he chose not to.

Darren was a massive, perfect specimen of a man. He was tall, muscular, good looking and super intelligent.

His hair was thick and dark and perfect. His eyes were blue and bright. He was twenty years old and the perfect man. There was just one issue to being the perfect man. He didn't consider himself to be one. He was nonbinary. Adam didn't even really know what that meant, and boy had Darren struggled to come to terms with his father's ignorance and stupidity.

Adam blamed the death of his wife for scrambling the boy's mind. Darren found this theory the biggest insult in the world and confirmation of his father's Neanderthal understanding of anything.

Adam ditched the toilet roll and the newspapers and ran up the stairs as fast as he could. Heart pounding. Fear coursing through his body. "Darren," he gasped as he ran two steps at a time over the brown and orange paisley carpet he so hated.

He burst into Darren's room and there they sat, smiling with an arrogant look that Adam, despite being overcome with love and relief at that very moment, wanted to knock off their face.

"Ah! You knobhead," yelped Adam. "You scared the crap out of me. I thought you might have been dragged to the front by one of those hit squads."

"You know I'd never fight," quipped Darren.

"You might not get a choice," hissed Adam. "There's a war coming any day now. People are going to die trying to defend this country and it's only a matter of time before we're expected to take part. Especially you. You're twenty. Perfect soldier age."

"We don't acknowledge country as a concept," came a voice from behind Adam who leapt from his skin.

"Christ what the…? Annabelle, what the hell are you doing behind the door?" he moaned.

"Country is an outdated concept like Christ, hell, gender and many of your other simple-minded ideas," gloated Annabelle.

"How about a punch to your nose, you daft cow?" retorted an irate Adam.

"Yes. Violence is also an outdated concept of yours, as is a female connotation of a bovine," smirked Annabelle.

"For God's sake – will you please bog off, Annabelle, with your half-baked concept ideas? This is the real world. I'm not having you coming into my house and spouting this nonsense. My house. Is that a concept you understand?" Adam's emotions were getting the better of him.

"Actually no," replied Annabelle. "Wealth is simply a form of greed and should be eradicated. There is sufficient for all humans to be treated entirely equally. And it's A, not Annabelle. I denounce any gender-based identity given to me by my uneducated parents."

"They were educated enough to piss you off to come and live here for free on my nasty wealth and greed though eh," growled Adam. "It's because of you that Darren's gone all weird."

"Cain," said Darren. "I denounce my gender-based identity too."

"And yet you've picked a boy's name, you halfwit," laughed Adam.

"I've picked a nonbinary name," came the reply.
"Haha. Well, name me one girl called Cain and we'll
    agree," challenged Adam.

"You just don't get it do you, Dad. There are no girls, no boys, just people. I've chosen a name that I want and you will call me Cain," they said.

"I bloody will not. Your mother called you Darren.
Remember her?" said Adam through gritted teeth.

Darren immediately burst into tears and stormed out of the room slamming the door behind him and leaving an uncomfortable Adam face to face with an angry-looking Annabelle.

"You did that to Cain," Annabelle growled. They stood aggressively; hands on hips over their tie-dyed pale blue jeans which were rolled over massive-soled plastic black boots. Together with their peroxide shaved head and oversized hoody, they looked positively threatening, despite a beautifully angelic face, with Disney princess eyes extenuated by dark black eyeliner.

Adam placed his head in his hands and groaned. They were right he just didn't get it. None of it made sense to him. He came from a time where there were boys and girls and everyone went to church and prayed to God and that pretty much was that. He didn't like this modern world but, above all, he was scared half to death about what future beheld these young people with their modern thinking if the powers from the East took control. Eastern ideas were brutal. He was not sure Annabelle would even get the chance to claim not being a female when some hairy-arsed depraved soldier came to discuss the matter with her.

He shook his head in her direction and left. He slowly walked downstairs with his thoughts all over the place. He picked up the Izal and smiled as he thought of the beautiful girl next door. 'She's definitely a girl,' he mused as he stepped over the ditched bundle of papers.

He didn't notice the front page headline which said, 'Nuke Them.'

Chapter 2

God Save Us

After a small and sensible meal of chicken and leaves, or in the case of Darren and Annabelle, leaves and more leaves followed by a significantly lengthy lecture on Adam's heinous meat-eating slaughter-of-innocents habits which led to Adam yelling at them about where the hell they thought the glue that held their precious iPads together came from, Adam left to the kitchen to wash the dishes and tidy up.

He wondered if he should ask the girl next door on a date but where do you go for a date when the city has fled underground, food is scarce and your son and his friend are so hostile you don't even care to be in the house near them yourself, let alone invite a date around?

Maybe he could bake a cake and go to hers. The dying granny was a downer but he might not be alive in a week to get another chance.

He was suddenly wracked with guilt. He had loved his wife with all his heart and though he knew he had to move on he still felt like he was betraying her. He hoped God would understand. He hoped that his wife would understand. He just wanted, no needed, to feel happiness once again and he felt sure that girl was the answer.

There was just the small issue of World War Three to contend with first.

He prayed.

"Lord forgive me," he started.

"Why what have you done?" said Darren from behind, startling him.

"If you must know I was thinking about asking the girl next door on a date and was seeking forgiveness from

God and your mother," whispered Adam.

"Do it. She won't mind. She's not in heaven looking down. There's no such place. No God, no heaven, no hell and no Mum. She's dead, Dad. Dead. We miss her. We do. We love her. We always will. But you need to be happy. I need to be happy. The person next door loves you. Anyone can tell that. They're beautiful and smart and funny…"

"And lonely," interrupted Adam.

"…and lonely. Like you," continued Darren. "And have you seen their boobs? Phew!" Darren gesticulated with his hands to his chest.

"Oh so you notice things like that do you?" mocked Adam. "I thought you were a woman called Colin now."

"Cain, Dad, Cain. And I'm not a woman there's no such thing. I'm not a man. There's no such thing. They are just societal labels designed hundreds of years ago to make people conform, pay taxes and fear gods. Like yours."

"I don't fear God," said Adam.

"Yes you do. Otherwise why are you asking their forgiveness for fancying the person next door? I love you, Dad. You're not going to hell for moving on from Mum. The nearest thing to hell you'll see is this war that's coming to greet us very soon." Darren embraced his father.

"Thanks, Darr… Cain. I love you too, son. Can I still call you son?" asked Adam with a laugh and he hugged his son. "Don't you think she's too young for me? What is she, late twenties?"

"Probably in her thirties, Dad," came the reply. "Maybe you should ask them the essentials like age, name perhaps and, of course, do they want children."

Adam stepped back and looked shocked. "I never even thought about things like children. I'm forty-six. I assumed you'd be having children next, not me but…" Adam nodded towards Cain's genital area repeatedly "…you know." He nodded again.

Darren laughed. "I'm of no gender, Dad, not nonsexual."

"Oh I just don't understand," moaned Adam. "The world has gone mad and I'm not sure I fit into it anymore. So you and Annabelle do… that… and might have children… wait don't answer. I don't want to know. I love you. I suppose I love her, I mean him, Annabelle, whatever she is, he is, they is… A. I love A too and as long as you're happy that's all that's important to me."

"Aw how sweet. You love me after all," said Annabelle who had sloped into the room. They were holding an iPad and nodded in its direction as they said, "Apparently the PM is going to do some sort of monster announcement on the telly in the next few minutes. I think we should watch."

In a super modern and stylish living room, designed by Adam's wife prior to her death, they waited at the television with nervous anticipation as the Prime Minister of the United Kingdom shuffled uneasily into her position in front of a mahogany rostrum over which was a carefully strewn flag of the Union.

Minutes later, an ashen-looking Darren turned off the television and with tears in their eyes looked towards Adam for some sort of hope or salvation.

Adam gulped. He was lost for words. 'Nuclear retaliation' spoken so forcefully by the elected leader of his country spun round and round in his head, overtaking any other thought he tried to process.

Annabelle screamed. A lung-filled primal scream that gurgled with phlegm and spit and shattered his already aching brain.

"Calm down, A," reassured Darren. "It won't happen.

They wouldn't be that stupid. It would mean the end of humanity. You can't just start attacking people with nuclear weapons, in defence or not. They will retaliate. The Americans will retaliate. That'll be that. It's a veiled threat so that this Eastern Republic lot about turn and leave England. It won't happen. It can't."

"I can't believe they've landed in England and are on their way to London," said Adam. "Oh God. This hasn't happened since William the bloody Conqueror."

"There is no God," said a suddenly stoic Annabelle. "If there was they wouldn't be about to allow the destruction of the Earth. Although they could always just rustle up a new beginning like last time of course."

Adam looked like he was about to explode before Darren intervened with a careful "Not the time" and a reassuring arm around Adam's shoulders.

"She's right," said Adam gazing unnervingly into nowhere in particular. "We have to fight. On the beaches, in the streets…"

"They're right," said Annabelle causing Darren to glare and shake his head in scolding.

"Nicked Churchill's speech that's all," Annabelle continued. "It's bollocks. No one will fight. No one wants to. Simply using some racist bigot's words from the past isn't going to do any good. We're people that are beyond fighting. We're much more advanced than that."

"Listen, sweetheart," started Adam.

"I'm offended by that," interrupted Annabelle.

"I don't give a steaming turd if you're offended," Adam continued. "Calling Churchill a racist is offensive to me. He's the reason you're allowed to come up with all this nonbinary crap, ponce around sponging off the state and wear your hair like you do without being dragged into some gulag. You and your ways are highly offensive to me. You saying there's no God, no Jesus, no religion, is highly offensive to me. I've got news for you, honey. These horrible bastards that have invaded our country don't care about you being offended, your rights, your pet bunny's rights or whether you want to be called a letter instead of your name. They're going to kill your arse or worse, keep it alive and do whatever they want with it. Now she may have used someone else's old speech but the sentiment was dead right. We have to fight for our freedom. Your freedom. So that you can be who you want to be."

"They," growled Annabelle from behind her hand.

Adam ignored this pettiness and moved on. "She said that any abled person should report to their nearest police station immediately to be… conscripted I guess."

"There's no way they'll make me fight," said Darren. "Nor me," Annabelle chipped in.

"What, so you're just going to sit here and let us lose and then nuke the hell out of everything?"

"Violence is simply not an option," said Darren. "I would rather die."

"Well you will die, you moronic idiot. You are unbebastardlievable," shrieked an increasingly upset Adam.

"Whatever will happen will happen," said Darren. "Neither you nor I nor A, nor anyone else, can change the future. You have to let it pan out the way it wants to."

"Of course you change the future," Adam snorted. "Or you can at least try."

*

It didn't matter that he tried everything from screaming to pleading. It didn't matter that he cried and hugged and begged some more. At seven am the next morning Adam hugged his son one last time and left his home to join a fight he thought he wouldn't win whilst Darren and Annabelle stayed behind steadfastly refusing to harm another living thing.

He turned left and headed in the direction he had come from the previous day. In the distance he heard a loud bang. The war was here. It had arrived already. He turned to have one last look at his home. In the front first floor window of the house next door stood the girl. She was red eyed and crying heavily. She looked so forlorn and yet she mustered him a smile and blew him a kiss.

He smiled and moved on before stopping again. He wondered if she had looked so distraught because the old lady had died. He turned again but she was no longer there. Another loud explosion rocked him from his thoughts and he jogged onwards towards an uncertain future.

Chapter 3

War

Seeing someone's head blown apart by a bullet to the face hadn't been the horrifying experience Adam had expected it to be. Rather than terrifying, it was tranquil and slow and calm. The screaming white noise of war dampened everything into a surreal, almost floaty episode at its most brutal times and he quickly realised this was how soldiers managed to function through such harrowing conditions.

A loud crack close to his head made him snap from his dreamlike existence and plunge to the floor as a hail of bullets ripped into a wall where had been standing.

"Jesus wept," was about all he could manage to say before he was grabbed by the collar and dragged into an alley by an alarmingly strong arm.

The arm belonged to the only real soldier in the platoon. Tall, dark and muscular with tight-cropped dark hair and a beaky nose that didn't match his strong square jaw, Second Lieutenant Jonjo Linton had been hastily promoted from Lance Corporal to the officer rank due to the significant massacre of existing officers and the need for someone with any sort of combat experience to command butchers, bakers and candlestick makers. Linton's four years a soldier and peacekeeping mission following the Ukraine conflict sufficed. Needless to say, he was a significantly better soldier than those he commanded but the fact that Adam was still alive, when so many of his compatriots were not, proved he too was holding his own.

Now he was grateful to the arm of Linton and as he crashed into an ancient stone archway under a hail of bullets he took stock of his situation.

Adam, Linton and three others, one of whom looked like he was at least grandad-age and was spurting blood from his shoulder and whimpering as he drifted in and out of consciousness, were hunkered down in the archway unable to move either forwards or back.

Through the smoke and rubble Adam saw his new friend Bill. Bill was a fit, sixty-year-old accountant with grey curly hair and bifocal spectacles who had done two years in the Territorial Army in the 1990s: skills suitable enough to make him Sergeant. This was one ramshackle, inadequate army and Adam knew it.

He barely knew how to fire his gun and struggled with the safety catch every time he needed to. Twice he'd had to seek help to change the magazine which had a tricky little mechanism that he couldn't properly fathom. He'd been afforded two days of training before being thrown into bloody conflict and his twenty shots on a makeshift range proved he couldn't hit a cow's arse with a banjo anyway.

Adam had lost his bayonet on day one of being on the front line because he hadn't connected it properly and had missed his uniform fitting due to the warehouse being destroyed by a ballistic missile, so as a consequence was wearing a khaki military-issue shirt under an oversized navy anorak with the badges removed, blue denim shorts and a pair of white Nike Cortez, possibly the slippiest training shoes ever to have been invented. He cursed Bill Bowerman for not adding his waffle to the design for a bit of grip.

His twenty-two-year-old, perfectly toned, athletic-training PTI, strutting about in her pristine white vest top and red shorts, had failed to grasp either the complete lack of basic skills, fitness or capability of her new recruits, nor the genuinely heroic desire to save their families as being the only thing outweighing their intense fears of failure and the future. She screamed abuse and hurled insults whilst she flexed her giant biceps, making a butterfly tattoo on one appear to flap its wings. Adam had empathised that maybe she could see that himself, Bill and Doreen, Bill's ever-loving wife, were the combat equivalent of Dad's Army's softer, more incompetent, older brothers and sisters and, being the PTI's only hope of living beyond the new moon, he would probably have screamed insults too.

Blessed Doreen who was a recently retired old school nursery nurse with a grey bun tightly crafted onto the top of her head, red-rimmed spectacles balanced on the end of her nose and a white knitted wool cardi, had lasted less than three minutes of fighting. Her only achievement in this war was to use up a significant amount of the enemy's ammunition after being hit with so many shots that no one even went to check that she was alive because it was obvious to anyone she was not.

Bill, having been married to Doreen for nearly forty years, witnessed the brutal execution of his wife but had refused to buckle, or show any emotion whatsoever. "The mourning can wait until we've won," was all he said on the matter.

Overnight, merely a mile or two from Adam's home, they had been dug into a street barricade of old furniture, ovens, doors and even a small tricycle which was all piled haphazardly between a Tesco Local that was missing a window and clearly stripped of all stock, except for a pile of discarded Lottery scratch cards that had become suddenly worthless, and a Greggs bakery which looked tatty and bleak when devoid of a window full of cakes and cookies.

Adam had seen Bill quietly sob into his green Berghaus jacket hood, bravely hiding his grief from watching eyes. Adam respected this old warrior with all his heart and prayed that they would seek solace in their losses one day.

Three days later, after intense fighting and more casualties on both sides than anyone was able to count, the news broke that the Eastern forces had broken through defensive lines and were fast approaching London. Adam still couldn't comprehend what was occurring. This was Great Britain. People didn't invade and certainly everyday folk didn't battle it out on the streets like animals. There was a modern technological army for this type of situation, although he had watched from home as tensions rose and the army was deployed into Europe as each country began to fall.

He didn't fully understand. China, North Korea, India, Russia, Iraq, Iran and a whole host of smaller countries, which he had heard of but had no idea where they were in the world, had begun collectively annexing surrounding countries. The USA huffed and puffed but did very little. Britain, France, Germany and the likes did likewise until it was too late. The fall of Japan had been a real eye-opener.

One by one, countries fell to these collective forces and now it was the turn of the UK and here he was. Adam – Defender of Nations.

Very soon, in the midst of a chilly afternoon, Adam and the others found themselves in the heat of their own battle. What was once a commercial shopping area in Finchley was now a battleground. Giant holes in the road raised mounds of tarmac and concrete that looked like jagged osteoderms running down a dinosaur's back. Shops were rubble, and rubble was hiding places for terrified citizens. Smoke and dust filled the air from raging fires, here there and everywhere. A once beautiful oak tree lay felled across the way with its leaves just beginning to turn from lush green to rust brown. A crumpled bus shelter and what was once a car lay crushed beneath the mighty trunk. A row of shops remained relatively intact and a defiant Union flag rippled from the Georgian architecture at an overhead window.

Bill was crouching in the centre of the road behind a smoking yellow Renault Clio and was clearly wounded. There was no apparent way to get to him without committing an obvious suicide on route.

Adam looked at a hand grenade attached to the ill-fitting ballistic vest he had found earlier. He really had no idea how to use it and was hoping that pulling the pin and hoying it in the general direction of the enemy like he had seen in the movies was what he should actually do in real life. He visualised the moment. Pin in hand, explosion ten yards away.

A massive explosion shattered both his eardrums and his grenade daydream and threw him flat on the floor. He scrambled back to his feet, clutching at his eyes to try and scrape out the dust and grime. His vision reappeared before his hearing. Linton was in his face yelling instructions. He could see his mouth moving but could only hear a high-pitched scream in his head.

Adam looked around and his heart sank. The Clio was no longer there and neither was Bill. In its place was a large crater, black scorch mark and fire. Adam fought back the tears. Bill wasn't the first new friend he had lost but it didn't feel any easier.

Maybe Darren was right. Maybe he should have just stayed at home and refused to fight for the future of his child.

A smack to his shoulder sprung him from his doldrums. "Glb glb glb argh glb," Linton mumbled whilst facially appearing to scream.

"I'm deaf," yelled Adam.

"You're not dead," screamed Linton in his face, suddenly perfectly audible.

"I'm deaf," repeated Adam realising that it was a futile comment because he no longer was.

Linton bashed Adam to his chest removing the little bit of breath he'd been able to muster through the smoke and dust.

"You're not dead. You're alive," yelled Linton. "Deaf," shouted Adam, "I'm deaf. But I'm not now so forget it."

"What?" replied Linton.

"Just pissing well tell me what you were saying," hollered an exasperated Adam.

"I can't hear you," hollered an exasperated Linton. "There's a kid over there. Kid there. Kid... There!" He pointed towards an apartment block.

In the midst of the concrete grey of the dust and rubble of war stood a girl. She was no more than twelve years old and looked remarkably like Hayley Mills in her film *Pollyanna*. Wearing a perfectly clean yellow and white lace dress with white knee socks and large yellow bowed ribbons in her golden plaited hair, she shone like a beacon through the grime like the first daffodils of spring bursting through the snow. The girl was smiling and waving in the direction of the beleaguered soldiers.

"What the hell is she doing there?" gulped Adam. "We've got to get to her."

"We've got to get to her," said Linton.

"It's a suicide run," said the soldier to Linton's left. Adam didn't know him well because the guy was mostly an aloof sort but he knew he was called Boydy, was in his fifties and had been a postman for thirty years.

Adam noticed Boydy's barbed wire tattoo of the Pamela Anderson era around his bicep and it occurred to him that his entire platoon other than Linton had been made up of old men and women. The young, like Darren, were conspicuous by their absence.

"I'll go," said Linton. "I'll get her."

"No. I'll do it," volunteered Adam. "You're needed more than me to run this lot because, let's face it, this is a no return kind of a job. Even if I get to her we're not making the return run together."

"You're a brave man," said Linton.

"You're a nutter," added Boydy helpfully. "It's a suicide run. You won't make it past the first five yards."

"Well you're welcome to go in my place," said Adam.

"Not a chance sunshine," came the reply. "It's a suicide run. You're going to die."

"Well I can't just leave a young lass out there to get killed can I?" screamed Adam and with that he presented his rifle, fired off a couple of shots to nowhere in particular and began to run.

"God be with you," called Linton after him.

Adam ran faster than he had ever run before. His chest heaved and his knees throbbed, but he pumped his arms and just kept going.

Bullets rained all around him and he felt the heat as one ripped past his face, closer than he ever knew or could have expected not to hit him.

He closed his eyes and concentrated on his breathing.

Then he stumbled over some rubble and nearly fell. "Jesus Adam," he said out loud. "You're not a bastard Jedi."

He opened his eyes, regained his footing and kept going.

Close now, he noticed that Pollyanna appeared to be transparent. Was he dreaming? Was he dead?

A massive cracking sound split the air and smoke and dust from the ground engulfed him as searing pain shot through his entire body.

Then there was darkness. Then white. 'Yeah I'm dead,' thought Adam.

Then he thought no more.

In that moment in time, he ceased to exist.

Chapter 4

Heaven

First, an unbearable pain wracked Adam's body to such a degree that he screamed through his veins and pores.

Then he was hot. Not painful hot but 'been on holiday to Turkey and sunburnt' hot.

'Pain. Heat,' thought Adam. 'Crap. I'm in hell.'

He always knew that kissing Veronica Chalmsworth on a drunken work night out one year into his engagement to his wife was going to come back and haunt him and here it was. Hell. It seemed harsh, he thought, but other than deliberately popping Tim Lines' football as a kid he couldn't think of anything else he had done wrong that might warrant an eternity in damnation. And Tim Lines was a bully. A hair-pulling, arm-punching, name-calling bully. He deserved to have his ball popped. Adam was doing his primary school a solid favour.

God's standards of behaviour were horrendously high to have landed him here.

Adam realised he could feel long soft warm grass under his body and he scrunched his back into it and smiled. The heat was relentless but not actually unkind and he slowly realised it was the beautiful warmth of the sunshine that sizzled his skin.

He nervously opened one eye and then shut it tight, fearful of what he might find.

Instead he slowly tried to move his arms and was pleasantly surprised that he could. He wriggled his toes and shuffled his legs. Everything was in one piece and he breathed a sigh of relief that half of him wasn't splattered over the streets of suburban London.

Adam felt about with his hands. Soft warm grass curled through his fingers. There was nothing else to feel. It made no sense to him and he considered it was probably prudent to open another eye and check what was going on.

As he was about to do so, a small portion of his hearing kicked in. The call of what sounded like an eagle shrilled into his brain. A distant breeze blowing leaves of trees. A waterfall. He could hear a waterfall.

Bravely Adam opened both eyes and looked around. There was no war. No fire. No smoke. No girl. No Linton. No death.

Instead he was engulfed in thick lush grass surrounded by large colourful blooms of red and yellow and pink like nothing he had ever seen before. Each petal was a blast of perfect colour and of a size and scale ten times more brilliant than he had ever seen in the front bit of the local M&S. The grass, which was the purest, perfect green and made of identical blades that danced from side to side where he stood, formed a small opening in a thick oak woodland and Adam was reassured by the sight of this stalwart British tree with deep riveted bark and curled leaves. And palm trees. There were palm trees! There were palm trees, oak trees and... lemon trees laden with fruit. Lush, bright, glossy lemons hanging in abundance right there.

Adam's eyes darted about. Oranges, apples, bananas, all growing side by side with oak trees. What was this place? He suddenly and automatically leapt to his feet and with his heart beating fast looked around.

"Haha," laughed Adam, more through nervousness than anything else. "Well I'm not in hell," he said aloud.

He looked at his surroundings in more detail. The grassy area was about fifteen feet square, with natural grass, though each blade looked like it had been carefully selected by the Wimbledon Lawn Tennis Association.

There was a bank of flowers on each side of the grass. Bright blooms of a type he did not recognise as anything he had seen before. They were massive and incredible and Adam felt certain they would win the Chelsea flower show in a heartbeat.

Beyond the flowers were the trees. It was miraculous to see them, so full of fruit at the same time.

It was unbelievably warm too, yet not unpleasantly humid, albeit clearly wet in places for such abundant growth to take place.

"This place is perfect," said Adam in wonderment as he gazed about.

He walked towards the flowers and tried to look beyond, towards the sound of the waterfall. The flora was so thick he could see nothing but lush green vegetation.

'This is some garden,' he thought.

He looked up and could see a bright blue sky with one perfectly formed, fluffy white cloud bobbing about in the blueness.

He looked down and looked at grass again. He saw his feet. Bare, sockless, lily white from the English winter feet were nestled in the lush green grass.

"I've lost my boots and socks!" he said aloud and, before he had time to even begin to think about how this could have occurred, realised he was trouserless too. He stared down at his nakedness. No underpants. No top. Nothing. He was entirely naked.

His immediate response was to dive for some sort of cover to hide his modesty from onlookers but he quickly realised there were no onlookers or easily accessible hiding places. Instead he simply stood staring at his manhood, so uncharacteristically on full display.

Despite that he had been in the depths of a violent and bloody war moments earlier, a Pollyanna lookalike apparition had come and gone, he had apparently died and come back to life and was now standing in a lush tropical yet seemingly British paradise; Adam's entirely male brain focused only on one thing. The size of his willy.

He wished he had manscaped because he was unpleasantly hairy and felt sure he was losing a couple of centimetres as a consequence.

He grimaced. The paunch of his stomach even obscured his view. He had let himself go following the death of his wife and he knew it. Now in all his naked glory he wished he had been working out for the last few years.

He jingle-jangled in an attempt to reposition himself into a longer-looking position and then he was struck with an incredible thought.

"Heaven," he said loudly. "I'm in heaven."

It was the only explanation. The nakedness. The warmth. The perfect garden. It had to be heaven.

Adam held his arms into the air and screamed "I'm in heaven" to the skies.

He wasn't. What happened next proved it very clearly to him.

Chapter 5

Hell

As Adam hailed the skies and declared himself in heaven, a bluebottle landed on his shoulder.

This was no ordinary bluebottle. This bluebottle was the size of a cat. As it landed on Adam it knocked him off balance and somewhat winded him. The bluebottle's wings vibrated against his face and it was like being slapped repeatedly by a table tennis bat. The buzzing was really loud, even to Adam's recently terrorised ears.

For a second or two, Adam was completely disorientated and had no idea what on Earth was going on: something which appeared to be happening to him with alarming regularity.

With the dawning realisation that he had been assaulted by a giant fly, Adam went into a full-scale arm-flapping freak out. He ran. He screamed. He flapped. He jumped around. He screamed some more.

The bluebottle stayed steadfastly to his shoulder slapping him heartily with every wingbeat.

Adam's brain was failing him woefully as to what to do about this scary monster beast on his shoulder and then came up with just the tactic required.

Adam threw himself into the air as high as he could muster and then flipped his legs out behind himself so that he returned to the ground horizontally. And fast.

With a massive thud, Adam bellyflopped to the floor. The wind smashed from his lungs and he gasped for air through his grass-filled mouth and nose. The fly would be crushed.

It wasn't.

The bluebottle hovered a couple of inches above

Adam's head, deafening him.

Adam groaned and rolled onto his back.

The bluebottle proceeded to land on his face. Then spewed.

Disgusting green and yellow lumpy slime sloshed over Adam's face and neck and slid towards his gasping mouth.

Adam slammed his lips together tight but internally heaved, repulsed at what was happening to him.

He swung his left fist at his own face with all the power he could muster and punched the blue bottle in the head. It buzzed loudly before taking to the skies.

Adam, still with lips clenched, dared not take a breath. Then his face began to burn. The acidy vomit was cutting into his skin with alarmingly painful ease.

Adam flipped again and smashed his face into the grass. He swished back and forth, rubbing harder and harder, and eventually the pain stopped sufficiently for him to take a breath and collapse into a heap.

No sooner had he done so than he heard a slight buzz and leapt to his feet looking frantically around and flapping his arms. It was a false alarm and he sighed a huge sigh of relief.

'What the hell is this place?' thought Adam who, unbeknown to him, now had a bright red burnt face covered in mud and grass stains.

'Think, Adam,' thought Adam.

He looked at the facts. He had been fighting a war in the broken and bloody streets of London. The enemy had engulfed London and the threat from the Prime Minister had been to use nuclear weapons on anyone who did. He had seen Pollyanna. He had been engulfed in pain, then white, then here. He was inexplicably naked. Then a bloody massive dog crap eater had landed on him and tried to spew his face off.

"I've either been shot to death or nuked to death and I'm here in this heaven-like garden just with really really big flies," he said out loud. "Or hell maybe?"

Seconds later he changed his hell opinion from maybe to definitely.

The trees to his left rustled and gave him a start.

He turned, frozen solid, and stared into the greenery past the glorious flowers. There was something there watching him. Something big. Not a cat-sized fly. It was much much bigger than that.

Adam looked around for somewhere to run. No simple directions came readily to mind so he chose the most obvious which was the direct opposite to where whatever the giant thing that was watching him in the woods was.

He slowly turned and shimmied to his right as slowly as he dared. The leaves rustled and moved. The thing was creeping towards him.

"Aaaah, bugger," mumbled Adam before turning and running as fast as he could. For the second time in minutes, yet in weirdly entirely differing circumstances, Adam ran because his life depended on it.

Life-threatening or not, the thing that caught his attention was that his penis was slapping on his bare leg and he was still watching it as he left the grassy area and ran into the flowers. The ground changed from lush grass to sharp and rough undergrowth and Adam yelped as his shoeless feet crunched on first dried soil and then woodland sticks, brambles and nettles as he burst into the trees.

"Aaaaargh," he screamed as he ran but he didn't stop and nor did he look back to see if anything was chasing him.

If he had, he would have seen that something was chasing him, and that that something was a dog which was about the size of a bear but otherwise looked like a particularly aggressive cross between a German Shepherd and a Rottweiler.

Adam continued into the forest, yelping all the way because of his feet. He had cursed his Nike Cortez through his few days of fighting and now he would have given anything for them.

He ran until he could run no more.

This was because he was spreadeagled face first in a massive cobweb stretched fifteen feet between two lemon trees.

With all his might he pulled his face from the stickiness of the web. It was strong and thick and held his arms, legs and body tight.

"All I need now is a giant spider to come along and eat me," laughed Adam almost delirious with fear.

He followed this with "Ah no" as a giant spider suddenly came into his sight at the top of the web.

He thought it looked about the size of a micro pig though less appealing to hold and cuddle. The spider was black with beady green eyes across its head. Its eight legs were as thick as a drainpipe with wiry black hairs running down the back of each one. Two massive yellow fangs made it look like the spider was grinning at him. Perhaps it was because he was a sitting duck to be the next meal of the day.

Adam wriggled and writhed but the web seemed to be getting stronger with him more attached.

"Shoo," he yelped as loud as he could. "Piss off."

"Do you speak English?" shouted Adam for no reason whatsoever because it was obvious that the spider was a spider and didn't speak at all.

The spider continued to approach. Slowly. Slowly. Slowly it came.

Adam thought of Darren and hoped he had survived whatever had happened. He prayed to his God and calmly awaited his death.

"Oh bummer," he suddenly shouted. "I'm already dead. Now what happens?"

What happened was a massive German Shepherd Rottweiler bounded through the air, crashing straight through the web and gobbling up the spider all in one movement.

Adam was thrown from the web and crashed into an apple tree some ten feet away. He shot to his feet and then stood for a second, barely able to believe what he could see with his own eyes.

The monster of a dog was on its haunches ready to pounce on him, its eyes fixed on his. Its teeth bared to the gums. It growled.

"Sit boy," shouted Adam more in hope than any expectation that anything would happen. When it didn't he consoled himself that it had been worth a try.

The dog growled loudly. Any second now he would attack.

Adam leaned to the floor, keeping his eyes fixed on the beast.

"Good boy," he whispered. "Or girl, or whatever," he added, remembering he would have been admonished by Darren for his masculine pronoun.

He shuffled his hand around the floor until his fingers rested upon the biggest stick he could find. He grabbed it and slowly retuned upright.

"Good boy," he whispered again to the increasingly agitated dog.

With an almighty throw, Adam tossed the stick away from both the dog and himself.

The dog bounded after the stick.

The surprise that this actually worked meant that Adam lost valuable seconds standing there in astonishment but he collected his wits and darted towards a large oak tree nearby.

The last he knew was that dogs didn't climb trees, or at least that's how he remembered it and he grabbed and pulled his way high into the mighty tree.

After being distracted by the stick, the dog leapt back into action and charged at where Adam was climbing as fast as he could.

It leapt through the air again, snapping its huge sharp teeth just shy of where Adam had just removed his leg. Adam tried to swear but only managed to whimper a strange squeak as he kept going up.

Midway up the tree he stopped. He considered going to the top but in five minutes in this place he had encountered massive killer flies, spiders and dogs. He had already heard the cry of a distant eagle and the last thing he wanted was to be attacked by a giant one of them while he was four hundred feet up in a tree.

He could see the dog from here too and he settled onto a large branch near the trunk. The dog paced around the tree, then up and down and eventually lay down at the foot of the tree and waited.

Adam was terrified. He looked toward the sky and noticed that though the sky was blue and bright there was a tint of orange creeping in and he wondered if hell had day and night and whether he was destined to spend eternity running from one scary monster to the next. One thing for sure was that he did not want to spend the night naked in a tree when even the insects were liable to eat him. Lord knows what unfathomable killers would come out at night time.

Adam suddenly realised that he had entirely recovered from the exertion of the run and climb. He wasn't out of breath and nothing ached. He had ached since his massive goalkeeper mate Dave Aspin had clattered through his back while collecting a cross, way back in the early

2000s. He breathed a deep breath. This place had good clear oxygen-filled air. He actually felt better than he had in years. 'Perhaps it's because I'm dead,' he thought so smacked his fist into the tree, which hurt. A lot. 'Perhaps not.'

He had expected hell to be a smoke-filled, hard-to-breathe kind of a place, much like he had experienced during the street fighting, but this place was lush. It was like heaven with hell's mates staying over.

He realised he was hungry. Apart from half a packet of Batchelors Super Noodles that morning he'd eaten nothing, and since the day he left home, he'd barely eaten anything that wasn't processed and full of salt.

He looked ahead and there was an orange tree laden with succulent oranges. To his left was the same with apples.

Adam shimmied along his branch until it was super thin and twiggy and began to bend heavily. He was still some way off the delicious fruits but close enough to be tortured.

He climbed back to his sturdy branch and began concocting a fruit-picking device by weaving twigs and sticks together until he had what looked like a long tweezer. In fairness it looked nothing like a long tweezer but that's what he had visualised in his head when he commenced the venture so he considered his scruffy branchy twig construction a success.

He shimmied back to the extremities of the tree with his device and leaned. The weight of his tweezer made him wobble and he had a horrific heart-in-the-mouth moment as he regained his balance.

More carefully he tried again, leaning as far as he dared. The tweezer was agonisingly close to an orange and twice he prodded it causing it to rock back and forth.

Again, he leaned out for another try. The orange shook

and fell to the floor.

The dog barked so loudly at this that Adam fair nearly shat himself and his jump caused him to rock and fall slightly. He dropped his tweezer device and grabbed for the sticks and leaves to stabilise himself.

"Bastard," screamed Adam and the dog barked again. Hardened to it this time Adam simply yelled back. "Piss off, you horrible mutt."

Annoyed, agitated and hungrier than ever, Adam began to return to his thick branch but, to his joy, he noticed his device was wedged a branch down in the leaves.

"Yessss," he cheered followed quickly by a, "screw you dog breath."

He quickly recovered the tweezer and set to his arduous task.

The next part of Adam's life, or death, or whatever it was, was the single most frustrating, infuriating, annoying and soul-destroying experience he had ever encountered.

Four times he was millimetres from grasping the juicy fruit and each time it fell from his grasp to new levels of cursing and swearing that would have made a sailor blush. Each time the dog barked and each time Adam hurled abuse at the animal with increasing hatred.

Those four times were the times he came close. The other six hundred and ninety-six attempts came nowhere near. He was so angry with the dog as oranges fell that he seriously considered climbing the tree and engaging the damn thing in a fist fight.

Attempt seven hundred and one bore success. The orange balanced precariously on the leafiest part of his device. Adam moved so slowly. His hands were shaking and the orange wobbled time and again as it inched nearer to his grasp. Two metres. One metre. Thirty centimetres. Twenty. Ten. Got it!

He cried. Adam clutched his orange tightly and cried and sobbed as a million emotions from his bizarre experiences washed from him in the glory of his success against the odds.

Then he dropped his orange.

Adam would never be able to tell how he did what he did next, but he did it.

As the orange spilled from his grasp, he instinctively darted after it, leaving hold of the tree branch. Adam fell headfirst, though his legs remained firmly hooked around the branch and he looped upside down, almost overtaking the falling orange with his momentum.

He grabbed at the orange with both hands as he passed. Years of slip fielding for Brockley thirds through balmy summer evenings suddenly proved useful and he palmed the orange firmly in both hands and then prayed that his legs would hold onto that branch.

They did.

Adam hung upside down by his legs, holding tightly onto an orange like it was the most precious thing in the world, high up in an oak tree with a rabid vicious monster dog below.

He had been in better situations without doubt.

Seven years ago Adam had done a sponsored press-ups and sit-ups event to raise money for the Parkinson's disease society. He had not done a sit-up since. His well crafted abs had long since disappeared under a few inches of flab. Now he needed them to do a return to action so that he could pull himself up.

To begin with, he couldn't move more than an inch and he actually laughed out loud at his patheticness.

"Come on, Adam," he yelled to motivate himself and with a mighty effort he managed a few inches of lift. He fell back upside down exhausted. "I'm screwed," he said.

After hanging upside down long enough to have a massive blood-flow headache, the additional oxygen feeding his brain came up with a splendid idea. He would eat the orange which would free up his hands then try and manoeuvre his way towards the trunk and then use his hands up the trunk to assist his awfully feeble sit-up action and get him back on his branch.

Pleased with himself, Adam began peeling the orange and instantly his already fragile mood shifted to despair.

The fruit of the orange was black and rotten. This really was hell.

Chapter 6

Home

Hanging from a tree and holding a rotten piece of fruit that had taken an age to retrieve tipped Adam to the brink.

He already considered that he was dead and in hell. It had to be hell. This place was danger, torture, tantalisation and frustration all hidden in a beautiful world of perfection. He was simply waiting for the devil to leap up and bite him on the arse and if that massive hound was him, then it might actually happen.

Short of anything profound to say to suitably match his circumstances, Adam simply yelled "bollocks" from the top his voice.

He threw the rotten orange away and it dropped quickly below him.

Adam didn't know it but the falling fruit plummeted through the tree branches, bouncing from one to another and changing direction as it went.

The massive dog had settled below into a snooze and was unconsciously growling with every breath.

The orange thumped the mutt right between the eyes. The dog leapt to its feet, startled and frightened, and, without having any idea what had occurred, made an immediate dash from the scene, keeping going until it felt safe.

From his upside-down vantage point, Adam saw the dog leave and he couldn't believe his fortune.

Not waiting for it to come back he quickly took his opportunity to make a move.

He scrambled towards the trunk by bouncing across the branch a leg at a time and made good progress, reaching his goal quickly. Adam scrambled his hands up the bark of the trunk lifting his body as he did so into a more upright position.

He scraped his body up the trunk for grip and, though it hurt and scratched a little, the bark made perfect traction. Very quickly he pulled himself parallel with his legs and yanked himself onto the branch with utter jubilation.

Then he fell.

Adam pretty much followed the route of the previous faller, the orange. He smashed into branches and bounced from one to another.

His awareness was stunted by each blow and after a short time he was limp, no longer trying to grab on as he fell. The last branch folded him over before he flipped and fell the last six feet to the floor onto his back.

Where he landed, the ground was soft with years and years of dead leaves and moss and but for this, every bone in his body would have been smashed. Instead he lay crumpled and unconscious in the undergrowth, partially covered by leaves.

An orange fell from the nearby tree, struck his chest and rolled to within a centimetre of his fingers.

*

When he awoke it was the next morning and the loud shrill of birds filled the air. Although he hadn't known anything about it, Adam had successfully navigated his first night in this strange place without being eaten, chased, melted or any other hideous outcome.

He was lucky. After first dark, a large mammal that looked remarkably like one of those snappy little dinosaurs in *Jurassic Park* had wandered past within a few yards of where he lay and yet had not noticed him.

Later a colony of giant ants, and by giant ants, these were ants the size of a rabbit, lined around him though concerned themselves only with collecting oranges and other fallen fruit before marching off.

Adam stretched and immediately winced. He was bruised and battered and the taste of blood made him realise his lips were stuck together with congealed blood. He quickly realised this was from a large cut above his eye which was swollen and split in the manner of having being punched by a heavyweight boxer. Other than that he seemed to be in one piece. He stood up and checked himself over. A pounding headache, small cuts and scrapes and he was black and blue but otherwise intact.

This was apart from his little finger on his left hand which was entirely missing. To lose a finger was very upsetting and for a long while he screamed when he looked at it for he could see the knuckle below a flap of open skin and congealed blood. He mooched around, looking for it but with no joy and eventually a weird noise from the trees made him give up the search.

Adam feasted on beautiful fresh fruit from the nearby trees and for the first time in this place felt a certain satisfaction. Albeit a fingerless morning, it was also an eventless morning and more and more Adam convinced himself that not only was he dead, but heaven and hell were muddled together on this place that looked like a perfect Earth.

Refreshed but short of anything that resembled a plan, Adam made the executive decision to keep walking, in the slight hope that he would bump into the Salvation Army or a robot finger surgeon or something equally helpful to him.

The going was remarkable. There was thick vegetation and trees in every direction, much like a tropical rainforest but with the added addition of the British countryside, minus cute furry animals such as squirrels and hedgehogs.

Adam regularly encountered giant insects and, following his earlier escape, carefully dodged numerous giant cobwebs which hung across his path with menacing occupants awaiting their prey and he became adept at hiding from any and every murmur of sound, just in case that sound belonged to some sort of giant killing machine that was liable to eat him.

Adam slept as high in trees as he dared without falling in his sleep, although, convinced he was already dead, he didn't apply much caution to his chance of survival should he fall.

Day became night four times and by the third he was no longer terrified of absolutely everything and he actually got a decent amount of sleep.

The sudden but infrequent noise of birds did regularly scare him half to death but he was reassured by the overhead thick canopy of leaves and convinced himself that if he couldn't see them, then they couldn't see him.

As convincing an argument as this was, it was desperately wrong. Particularly in the dark.

As the fifth dusk was descending, Adam looked around to find a suitable tree bed for the evening, blissfully unaware that above him an oily black crow-like bird, which was at least ten times bigger than he had ever seen before and had talons ten times longer than he had ever seen before, was circling; with Adam firmly in his sights for its dinner.

Adam had eaten well throughout and, having settled on a large apple tree with intercrossing branches that formed a nice bed for the evening, was feasting on a wonderful supper of summer fruits – raspberries, strawberries and gooseberries – gathered from the abundantly growing fruit crops around, when the crow decided it was its own meal time and darted through the branches and leaves towards him.

Adam heard the crow coming just in time to look up and see it swooping a yard from his face. He couldn't react other than to open his eyes wide and contort every muscle in his face into an ugly grimace.

The massive crow ploughed into Adam's forehead sinking one almighty talon into his recently healing eyebrow and another into his scalp above his ear.

Adam responded by making an indescribable noise that sounded like something someone might make when a giant crow had just harpooned their head. He fell backwards but instinctively grabbed the crow's back and wings as he did so. Using his momentum as he fell, he performed a backwards roll as elegantly as an eight-year-old girl from the school gymnastics team might, then dragged the crow from his grip and shook it with both hands so vigorously that large black feathers were strewn into the air.

Still holding the crow in both hands he hurled it into the trunk of a nearby larch tree. The crow flopped to the floor stunned. Adam frantically looked around for a stick big enough to club the flying bastard and laid his hands on a heavy branch which had a brilliant knuckle on one end, perfect for bird dispatching. He grinned as he wielded his club with vengeance in his eyes but as he approached, the giant crow had somewhat regained its composure and hopped off into the undergrowth.

"Yeah do one, dickhead," shrieked an overly excited Adam before laughing hysterically at his own words. "Did I just call a crow a dickhead?" he howled.

He felt his new wounds. He eye cut was reopened and blood poured down his face. He felt around above his ear and was astonished to find a giant crow claw still protruding from his head.

Exhaling he gripped the claw in his hand and pulled. "Aaaargh," he screamed, immediately letting go and dancing around in pain.

Four attempts to pull it out later, he decided to leave it sticking out and Adam retired to his slumber with blood pouring down his face and a giant talon in his head. Fifteen minutes later Adams bowel, confused by a sudden diet of fresh fruit and only fresh fruit and terrified by constant fear, gave up the ghost.

It was a rough rough night.

Adam thought it to be the second worst night of his life for toiletry issues, only beaten by the time he had taken part in a stag weekend 'curry hell' competition at the Rupali restaurant in Newcastle.

As morning broke and Adam rose, he found himself feeling remarkably chirpy given the circumstances. His claw head hurt marginally more than his eyebrow cut and marginally less than his bottom but he faced the day with a sense of excitement and determination to not let this hell beat him.

He feasted on fresh fruit for breakfast and then set off on his way.

A couple of hours into his most recent trek he heard the sound of falling water and began to run towards it without a care in the world.

He burst through the trees to find an oasis of tropical beauty. A large blue pool was surrounded by small rocky cliffs of crystal from which a wonderfully white waterfall flowed into the pool. Splendid flowers of yellow, red and pink surrounded the pool reflecting rainbows of colour in every direction.

For a second Adam stood open-mouthed at the beauty of this place and then, gathering his wits, looked around for killer crows, bees, flies, dogs or anything else he could think of.

He didn't think of crocodiles. Had he done, he may have avoided cannon balling into the water with gay abandonment, "woo hoo hoo"ing as he did so.

The splash of the water sent ever increasing circles to the edge of the pond and lapped against the watchful eye of a slumbering crocodile.

Adam splashed and sang in his luxury bath. The water eased his aches, cuts and bruises and was wonderfully warm. He cleaned away the blood from his matted body and washed away the war and the fear. He decided there and then that if he had to stay in hell, then this was the part of hell to stay in and he would remain here until it ever came to an end.

He flopped from his back to his front and bobbed on the water, allowing his head to drop beneath the surface from time to time. At first the claw stung like billy-o but eventually it eased and Adam resolved to pull the damn thing out once and for all soon.

He bobbed up and down, took a huge deep breath, closed his eyes and dropped under the delicious water, allowing the moisture to soak into his skin for as long as he could hold on. He splashed back to the surface and gasped for air, carefully wiping the water from his eyes.

As his vision retuned his heart sank. Floating half under the surface of the pool some thirty yards from him was the easily recognisable sight of seven crocodiles casually swimming towards him.

Almost paralysed with fear, Adam's brain went into overdrive frantically trying to distinguish the difference between crocodiles and alligators and most of all which one was likely to roll him to the bottom of the lake bed and eat his rotting carcass next week.

A little alarm in his brain suggested that in all likelihood the outcome was the same for both, so, having allowed the crocs to swim ten yards closer to him, he turned and began to swim to the shore as quickly as he could.

The cliffiest part of the pink and amber rock was closest to him and he figured that if he could make it up, the crocodiles wouldn't be able to climb after him.

Now Adam was no Duncan Goodhew but he could swim as well as the next person and he took off, confident in his ability to make the cliff. Olympic standard swimmer or not, it turned out that a crocodile was significantly faster than him and three yards from the rock, one pounced, leaping out of the water and crashing towards him. Adam rolled under the water and twisted away from the oncoming reptile in one movement and the beast overshot its prey and went straight over him. In a moment of extreme fortune, the crocodile's tail slapped him on the back of his shoulders and flung him forward towards the cliff, providing valuable space between him and the next croc.

Adam blasted through the remaining water and hauled himself onto the slippery rocks. With all his might he dragged his tired body up the rock face and lifted his knees into his chest just as a hungry crocodile leapt from the water snapping his jaws where Adam's legs had been moments earlier.

Adam shuddered and pulled himself onto a ledge, safe from any attack. For a moment he sat and observed the crocodiles swirling around in the water. As big and scary as they were, he noticed that they were normal, everyday crocodiles. They weren't overly big like everything else had been.

'Strange,' thought Adam, before continuing up the rock face and into the tangled woodland that grew from the top. 'Maybe crocodiles are scary enough to be in hell without any modifications?'

Despite drying quickly in the warm sun, he could not stop shaking and wandered aimlessly and lost, looking for anything that would help him in his survival or provide answers.

The land naturally began to climb and he scrambled his way through the trees and plants before the dense growth opened up into a wide grassy plain filled with wild flowers in sweeping rows.

He felt uneasy leaving the relative safety of the trees and being in such a wide open space but he had the gut feeling that he was at higher altitude and a brave assault of the grassy plain may afford him some reward, so he set off at a canter to make the experiment as quick as possible.

A short distance across the grass, Adam slammed the toe of his right foot into something hard which made him yelp, stumble and fall. He planted headfirst into the grass and rolled onto his side, clutching his throbbing toe end.

"Mother…" he screamed before immediately stopping in utter disbelief.

Wide eyed and already forgetting the throbbing pain in his bruised toe, he slithered across the grass to the point where he had tripped. Poking ever so slightly from the ground was the bevelled corner of a really old and severely rusted sign.

Adam pulled at the grass and weeds that surrounded it. A noise above made him temporarily roll onto his back and stare at the sky before he flipped again, excitedly revealing more and more of the sign.

As he pulled at clumps of grass and then dirt, words, barely distinguishable, were unsurfaced.

First an H. Next a T. Then an A.

More work was required to reveal an E and soon he was properly digging with his nails and hands to try and reveal more.

Feeling a well of anticipation that was almost unbearable, Adam scraped around the sign, trying to pull out the hidden portion, but it seemed deeply wedged in the hard mud.

It moved. So he waggled and wobbled and wiggled the sign to make it come loose.

It did, revealing a mud-covered rusted piece of metal with a ragged missing end. Frustrated that he couldn't see any more letters he quickly looked around and after a small search he fetched a large yellow fruit that he did not recognise and squelched it onto the sign. He rubbed up and down with a clump of grass and the mud dissipated.

Adam stared in disbelief at the faded rusty letters that were barely visible on this ancient sign.

'MPSTEAD HEATH' read the letters.

It didn't take Sherlock Holmes to work out it had once said 'Hampstead Heath' but Adam simply couldn't believe it and spent the next twenty minutes or so scratching at the earth in vain whilst trying to locate a further H and A just to be certain.

'Hampstead Heath' ran through his brain again and again. It made no sense.

Adam eventually gave up his search and remembered his original plan had been to venture across the grassy plain. He set off once again on his quest.

Some five minutes later, Adam stood gobsmacked looking at the view.

He could see a winding blue river from his vantage point but his eyes fixed on the broken and half derelict dome of a building way into the distance. The unmistakable sight of St Paul's Cathedral captured his unblinking gaze.

"This is London," said Adam to himself. "I'm home."

Chapter 7

Underground

For seven days, Adam battled his way through what increasingly felt like a jungle. He repeatedly got lost and many a time had to hide while some kind of potential predator wandered, ran or flew past.

He hid from what he thought was a large panther-like cat. He flapped at what was definitely a large cockroach and he booted a tiny furry little rodent creature across the forest floor after he had jumped with fright when it ran over his bare foot.

For a while he stood staring at the cute little furball, full of remorse for his actions. A large seagull shrilled in the moment and swooped down grasping the cutey in its mouth and flying away. Adam groaned and held his head in his hands, clumsily knocking the crow claw and cursing in pain.

For all that the distance wasn't great to where he was headed, Adam's sense of direction was awful and he regularly went further backwards than he managed to go ahead.

Eventually he reached the river he sought and couldn't believe the crystal clear waters he found. Fish of many species swam in abundance and he marvelled at their beauty. He looked at the water, the ruin of St Paul's and back to the water again. "This cannot be the Thames," he muttered. He had never seen clear water in it before and certainly not the riverbed. He dreaded to think what lay there now it was visible, no longer under mud and slurry.

It had been with a certain amount of disappointment that Adam had failed to find any other clue to his whereabouts or what had happened to his beloved city or how. He wanted to go home and check on Darren and Annabelle but it had taken an age to make it towards a giant landmark like St Paul's, such was his inability to see through the thick vegetation and, in any case, deep down he knew his home wasn't there.

Whatever this place was, be it hell or something else, Adam felt like he was in London town. Or at least a London town consumed by a jungle.

"Who the hell was that dude that kipped for ages?" asked Adam aloud, accustomed now to talking to himself. "Rick van Nistelrooy." He smiled, giving himself an imaginary pat on the back. "Maybe I slept for a long time?"

He pondered the idea. "Dreaming!" he suddenly declared. "Oh haah. I'm bloody dreaming. I must be in a coma." His mood soared. A coma was great news. Admittedly a coma was normally terrible news but given that he thought he was probably dead and in hell and was hoping for a better outcome than that, a coma was splendid.

He danced on the spot and spun around. "Coma and you know it is," he sang.

Suddenly completely resolved of all worry, fear and grief he marched on along the river edge.

He saw a distant bird and yelled at it, "Come and do your worst." He stood with his arms out in gesturing defiance, confident that it didn't matter what happened because he would eventually wake from his coma.

The bird stayed at a distance in the sky. "Mwa you scaredy cat," he shouted and laughed as he half skipped onwards.

It was amazing what the new found belief had stirred in him. He was confident and brash and rather than hide from noises, he embraced them full on. Remarkably no animal or insect came near the loud "coma" chanting naked hooligan that was marching along the edge of the jungle without a care in the world.

Eventually the river wound away and his route was unpassable and Adam had to return to the trees. It was a short time later his weird coma dream presented him with something exciting and he revelled in the drama.

Amongst the trees were the broken remnants of concrete that looked to Adam to have been a distant entrance to the London Underground. It was covered in vines and ivy and it took Adam a full twenty minutes to pull it away sufficiently to force his way into the hole that remained.

Pitch dark greeted him and he wondered what horrific monsters lay in wait for him before shrugging off the thought and yelling "Coma" as loudly as he could. His voice echoed and reverberated around making him think that he had entered a cavernous space.

Adam's eyes took an age to adapt to the darkness and barely so even then due to the lack of any light. Only what seeped through where he entered afforded him any sight and for a while he considered turning back into the forest, resisting due to a burning anger that resided in him from when he had lost his Oyster Card when he was fourteen and some horrible jobsworth security guard had wrongly accused him of leaping turnstiles. If this was the Underground, he was travelling Oyster Card free for once in his life, if nothing more than to get one back on that spotty prat who had caused him so much bother.

Scrambling along the wall of what definitely felt like the smooth brickwork of a tunnel, Adam shuffled step by step, determined to see where it led. Although he admittedly was a little alarmed at the lack of railway tracks under his feet, he was confident that he was making the correct decision to continue.

An hour later his confidence waned but he was so far

committed, it made no sense to turn back now.

Four hours after that, he was tired, hungry and was seriously regretting his shuffle in the dark. He kept going and going and going.

Eventually he slept. Lonely, and for the first time cold, he huddled his knees into his body and lay in the dark.

*

When he awoke, he did not have any concept of the time or how long he had been asleep. He noticed that something was seeping from the claw in his head and he hoped it was not his brain fluid. He ached. His feet hurt. His missing finger hurt like hell around the nail which wasn't there. 'How does that work?' thought Adam trying to touch the nearby wall with the ghost of his former digit.

Walking was near impossible because of the darkness but he shuffled carefully on. Mishaps, and there were many, were met with "Coma" shouts. Stumbles, falls, unexpected descents and climbs were regular and he suffered enough stubbed toes to make him wonder if they would have flat ends by the time he saw daylight again.

The darkness and the tunnel were relentless. On and on and on and never changing. On and on and on.

A scraping noise burst the silence but then there was nothing. His pounding heart was all Adam could hear now. Thump, thump, thump.

On and on and on he shuffled with tears pouring from his eyes and sweat and blood pouring from his body.

After forever, he thought he saw light and then moments later he knew he saw light. It was in the form of a large orange upside-down horseshoe, way in the distance. It seemed to flicker and fade but stayed present enough to give him momentum and he flogged along towards it, excited at last.

The horseshoe of light grew thicker and brighter the

closer he got and he became more and more excited as a consequence, eventually being able to walk more normally from the additional light it was providing.

Adam was still some distance away when he saw the source of the light. It was escaping from behind a giant object that was filling the tunnel. His heart skipped a beat. He was in the London Underground. He knew it.

Closer still he saw that a huge grey metal steel wall filled the tunnel from floor to ceiling, the light was escaping from cracks all around the edges where it joined the tunnel. There was a tall thin door in the bottom corner of the wall.

He approached it, exhilarated, and looked for a way in but there were none so, devoid of any better ideas, he knocked.

There was no reply so he knocked again, this time saying, "Rington's tea."

To his surprise and slight panic, there was a crunching noise from behind the door. This was followed by silence. He waited. Nothing.

He waited some more. The crunching continued but still nothing.

Frustrated now, he approached the door to knock harder but as he did so it flung open and engulfed him in light which dramatically blinded him.

As his vision fought against the burning brightness, Adam could see the shadowed shape of a human ahead of him. He was not alone. Wherever he was, he was not alone.

Chapter 8

Humans-ish

Playing the tough guy came relatively naturally to Adam.

He was the last of an age where men were men and the British stiff upper lip was unquestionably the answer to any issue. Darren had called it toxic masculinity. Adam called it British bulldog resolve.

Crying like a baby in the brightness, at the feet of the first human he had seen for way too long, Adam felt no more the bulldog but he didn't care. He crumpled to the floor in a wave of emotion and sobbed through snot and tears, making incoherent babbling to the saviour ahead of him. Exhausted and overwhelmed, he passed out.

*

When he awoke, he was laying in the softest, most comfortable bed he had ever found himself in. A white fluffy cover engulfed him and kindly tickled his skin. His pillows shaped his head and were warm and voluptuous.

A beautiful nurse smiled at him and he smiled back as he shuffled his head into that sublime pillow that was now caressing his head like a massage. The nurse was not just beautiful, actually, she was incredibly stunning. He opened his eyes wide and gazed at her. She had perfect bright blue eyes, olive skin with long brunette hair and snow-white teeth, caressed by the most beautiful lips he had ever seen. She was perfection. He couldn't ever remember seeing a more perfect woman.

She was wearing an all-in-one maroon skintight jump suit with silver strips that branched across it everywhere like veins. The jumpsuit was tucked into silver high-top boxing boots that said 'Nike' on them but had three stripes like Adidas.

'Curious,' he thought.

He looked around. The room was electrically lit; however, not with bulbs but with glowing strips of tape that donned the ceiling. Multiple machines silently seemed to be at work. There were no windows and he considered that strange.

"How you?" asked the nurse in English but in an accent he didn't immediately recognise. It was kind of American, kind of European but not really.

"I've never felt better," he said and it was true, "considering I've been in a coma."

The nurse stopped what she was doing and looked quizzically at him.

"I had some terrible dreams," Adam continued. "I presume the war was real. The war was real wasn't it? And... and then I was in light and it hurt but I woke up and got attacked by a giant fly. Then a dog. This massive bitch of a dog... oh sorry. I didn't mean to swear, love. I mean this dog attacked me and... oh I'm sorry. I didn't ask your name."

"Alexa." The nurse smiled.

"Like those bloody speakers," laughed Adam. "I bet you have a nightmare in your house every time someone says your name."

Alexa simply looked puzzled and said nothing. She leaned across him to check a tube that was attached to the back of his hand.

He noticed she was perfectly flat chested with a strong muscular chest as she leaned though her beauty was unquestionable.

"I feel great," said Adam. "Astonishingly great. Do you always feel so good after a coma? I suppose you're resting and repairing so why not?"

He suddenly remembered the crow claw and felt for his head. It was gone and there was no wound.

"Ha," laughed Adam, "I dreamed I had a crow talon stuck in my napper when I was coma'd out. And I lost my little finger on this hand." He held his left hand up to his face and examined his little finger. It was intact and as good as new, in fact he thought it looked better than new. The skin was less worn than his others and less wrinkled. It was also minus a mole he used to have on it.

"Replaced finger," said Alexa.

"Say what now?" questioned Adam, believing he'd misheard.

"Replaced finger," replied Alexa without a hint of frustration or emotion.

Adam stared at his little finger and moved it back and forth. 'Maybe she's foreign and can't understand me,' he thought.

At that moment the door into the room burst open and in walked three people.

Adam was horrified.

All three people were identical replicas of Alexa, meaning there were four of the same woman in the room. Initially Adam relaxed and sank back into his bed, safe in the knowledge he was still in his coma after all and must be close to waking up in the hospital, but one of the Alexas walked up and grabbed the covers, completely removing them in one motion.

Adam wasn't especially shy but in front of four of the most beautiful quadruplets that could possibly exist, he instinctively recoiled his very naked body, covering his dignity with his hands and arms.

"Hey," he shouted, "some privacy please."

One Alexa grabbed his arms and pulled them away from his body, whilst a second pulled his legs apart.

The three new Alexas stared incredulously at Adam.

Original Alexa began pointing at Adam like he was a painting in an art gallery and she was the curator.

"Penis and descended testicles. Hair," she explained and then lifted Adam's penis and flicked one of his testicles with her fingers.

Adam was being held tight by these freakishly strong women and couldn't move and was just beginning to shout "Hey leave me alone!" when the flick occurred so he barely managed the "hey" as the wind was taken from his lungs and pain engulfed his body to such an extent he nearly passed out.

The Alexas were shocked at this reaction so did it again. Harder!

The pain was unbearable and Adam sank back into unconsciousness.

He awoke to find himself snuggled in the warm of a beautiful bed. He opened an eye and was relieved to see he was in a basic white unfurnished room but was marginally worried when he noticed the strip lights of tape were the same as those from his latest dream.

He had no tubes or wires and there was no equipment in the room. He breathed a sigh of relief. Adam checked his head and there was no claw. He checked his finger and, though still looking remarkably new, it was intact.

He winced at the thought of everything he had dreamed and shuddered a couple of times.

"That was weird," said Adam as he pulled back the covers to stand and explore. He stopped and looked in horror. He was wearing an all-in-one jumpsuit with silver veins.

Wide eyed and uncertain what to do next, Adam sat bolt upright.

"Crap the bed," he said and then almost did as a blast of electric current zapped through his entire body completely disabling him.

"Hell's fire." A second blast took him down again. "Jesus…" Then a third blast.

Exhausted and confused, Adam lay in the bed. His brain very quickly realised that it was the suit that was electrocuting him so he scrambled and twisted to try and remove it. He couldn't. It was somehow fastened up his back but he couldn't work out how.

The door opened and in walked Alexa the ball flicker. Adam instantly covered his family jewels and looked sternly at the beautiful woman.

She smiled. Her beautiful smile melted him and he automatically relaxed against his will.

"Excuse me," Adam asked. "Are you Alexa?" Alexa replied in the affirmative.

"Are those other ladies calle...?" he began to ask but a blast of electricity from his suit took him down.

"Aaargh. What is happening to me? What's that for?" yelled Adam before a further blast of electricity took him down again.

He whimpered and rolled on the bed.

"Please tell me what's happening, Alexa," whispered Adam.

"Profanity outlawed," Alexa replied. "Aggression outlawed."

"But I didn't even swear," argued Adam. "And I wasn't aggressive." He felt himself getting annoyed and then quickly calmed himself down through fear of being annoyed being outlawed.

"Used profanity," said Alexa calmly. "Aggressive," they continued.

"But I didn't..." Adam began to argue and then decided on a different approach. Very nicely he asked, "Please can you help me remove this suit?"

"Removal suit outlawed," came Alexa's curt reply although it was delivered with a stunning smile which, to a degree, softened the bad news.

As politely and pleasantly as he could, Adam asked,

"Please can you answer some questions for me?"

"Yes." Alexa smiled.

"Was I in a coma?" asked Adam.

"No," answered Alexa.

"Am I dead?"

"No."

"Have I been dead?"

"No."

"So I've not been in a coma?"

Alexa delivered a warm smile and replied, "Asked already. No."

"What's the deal with the suit?" queried Adam.

"No deal."

"I mean what is the situation with the suit?"

"No situation."

Frustrated by the answers and the complete lack of any emotion in the delivery of Alexa's answers, Adam composed himself and asked again. "Please can you tell me what the suit is, how it works and why it's outlawed to remove it?"

The answer was so in depth that it blew Adam's mind. It was like a physics lesson, a chemistry lesson, a biology lesson and more complicated maths than he ever knew existed rolled into a little bit of home economics. Alexa stared blankly as if reading the information from the back of her eyes, maintaining a wonderful smile throughout. What Adam managed to gather from the hour-long delivery of information was that the suit was made from plants that were grown underground and powered by some sort of electro-thermo-chloroplast blah blah blah stuff that came from the lights but ultimately the sun. He simply hadn't been able to keep up with the information but he reasoned that that he was in a government facility which had developed some kind of electrical power generated by the sun above in the manner that plants did the same.

'Clever stuff,' he thought, and wondered why it hadn't been rolled out across the planet if global warming had been so important.

This thought meant he missed some of the next bit about why it was outlawed to remove the suit and Adam had to ask again.

Alexa answered with exactly the same words making him believe she was reading it from somewhere. "955 decided all humans comply Earth Convention legislation wear suit enforce legislation."

"So the suit is a law compliance device?" queried Adam. "Is that why it zapped me? But I didn't break any laws. Swearing is not a law. I got blasted a few times for nothing there. What's 955?"

"Year," replied Alexa.

Adam's mind turned over trying to make sense of what that meant but he let it go because he had too many other questions.

"There were four of you," he said. "All the same. Are they your sisters?"

A sharp blast of electricity made him scream. "Aargh. What the hell?" Another blast.

Adam yelled "Stop it" but another blast flattened him. He rolled in pain for a second recovering his composure.

"Look, lady…" he began, but a further blast hit him again.

"Aargh, I don't understand what's happening," whimpered Adam.

Alexa answered coldly whilst delivering a killer smile. "Pronoun, religion, aggression, pronoun."

Adam was simply shell shocked so remained silent while he thought and Alexa beamed a most beautiful smile.

"Alexa, what is happening?" Adam eventually asked

carefully.

"Clarify question," came the curt reply delivered with oozing charm.

"I'm confused," continued Adam. "I don't know what's happening, where I am, who or what you and your, err, colleagues are. I don't understand why the suit keeps electrocuting me. I don't know if I'm dead, dreaming, comatose, or what. I just… I just don't know what's happening or why."

Alexa smiled as she spoke and he couldn't help but feel reassured.

"You old aged living human male. DNA confirmed. Conscious. Healthy. Six cancerous cells. Heart life seven years without intervention. Brain deterioration 12%. Bone deterioration 17%. Other major organs functioning 67–82%. Recommended destruction under paragraph 56. In Zone 2 Province 10. Circus."

"Woah," interrupted Adam. "Circus? As in Oxford Circus the station? And did you say I have cancer and only seven years of heart life?"

Alexa was just about to continue when Adam interrupted again.

"Recommended destruction. What the hell does…" A burst of electricity shot through his body.

"Bastard!" he shouted and was electrocuted again.

"Continue," he prompted Alexa to go on as he slumped into the bed deflated.

"Seven years' heart life, six cancerous cells, destruction recommended," Alexa repeated.

"And I'm not old aged. I'm mid-forties," interrupted Adam defiantly.

Alexa continued, "Recommended lifespan functioning human twenty-five years. Paragraph 56 instructs self-destruction end twenty-fifth year."

Adam interrupted again.

"Right wait. I'm not getting any of this. Let's do this one at a time. Where am I?"

"In Zone 2 Province 10. Circus."

"Does that mean Oxford Circus? Piccadilly Circus? Am I in London?"

"The origins of Zone 2 are thought to be an important historical metropolitan area known as London."

"Historical?" questioned Adam. "That makes no sense. It has history for sure. Tower of London and all that. Zones and Provinces makes no sense. Have the Eastern forces set that up already and started removing city names? Hey maybe I've been unconscious for a long time."

Alexa simply looked beautifully at him and did not reply.

"Alexa," asked Adam, "what year is it?"

"955. Nine hundred and fifty-five A.D." She smiled back at him.

"955. I'm in the middle ages? That makes no sense. 955 Anno Domini?" Adam confirmed.

Alexa smiled and replied, "A.D. After Destruction."

Chapter 9

History of the Past

Although it was excruciatingly difficult to deliver for Alexa, and worse to understand for Adam, together they discussed the past.

Alexa seemed able to read the information from behind her staring eyes and as such was able to deliver detailed recorded accounts. Adam's constant interruptions, corrections and bellows of laughter, to what were clear inaccuracies, significantly delayed the story, although Alexa was able to listen to his remonstrations without emotion or frustration and continued unhindered as if his opinion or knowledge meant nothing to her. Adam was probably more perplexed than before once he had heard this story:

On the 18th June 1945 at Waterloo, a great war between the societies of the East and the West culminated with the destruction of everything by a series of nuclear explosions.

The West was made up of powerful and aggressive lead countries called the United States of America, Great Britain, Germany, France and Belgium. Germany was the strongest of these countries and headed up a huge landmass named Europa.

The humans of these countries were religious fanatics following a historic God from two thousand years previous named Jesus Christ. In spreading Jesus' words of love and peace, the humans had killed millions of people enforcing it.

The great leader of Europa was a powerful King named Elvis. Elvis had a Queen named Elizabeth and together they reigned for a hundred years. At first the

United States of America were unsure as to whether to follow the Jesus Christ religion and began to resist but Elvis invaded the country with an army known as the beetles, and these beetles tortured young people, making them scream and collapse.

Europa had three military generals: Einstein, Adolf Hitler and Napoleon. Napoleon was famous for torturing humans and they were known to pull their bones apart by hand with their great strength.

Each time a nation of people was converted to the religion, great games were held and champions were celebrated by lavishing vast wealth upon them. A huge hero named Kevin De Bruyne was the biggest champion. They were nicknamed "The Rock" such was their physical stature. Pictures of De Bruyne holding a golden hand, gripping the Earth which symbolised their control of the planet, still existed and were held in the Library of Historical Artefacts.

Elvis and Elizabeth waged a religious-led war upon the peace loving countries of the East such as Russia, India, China and Korea. The Eastern countries had great pacifists named Mahatma Gandhi, Nelson Mandela, Teresa, Stalin and Vladimir Putin and resisted the religious xenophobia forced upon them for years by means of peaceful protest.

Mandela was actually captured by the West and incarcerated for fifty years. Humans of the East gathered together and sang for Mandela's freedom whilst they were slaughtered in their masses by the West. Mandela famously managed to escape whereupon great celebrations in the East took place.

The West waged war on the East for ninety years and developed new and more terrifying weaponry and ways to kill the humans of the East.

In Germany, Einstein and Hitler eventually developed

the most horrific weapon. The weapon was known as the nuclear bomb. Einstein tested their development on a peaceful nation of people in the East known as Japan. The Japans had steadfastly refused to follow the religion of Jesus Christ and instead brought a gift of pearls to the people of the United States of America. The United States were horrified by the gift of pearls so Japan was selected as the target to test the new weapon.

Fifteen million innocent humans were obliterated instantly by the nuclear bomb. The resulting smoke and radiation clogged the atmosphere to such an extent that the radiation was blocked from escaping, causing the Earth to warm uncontrollably. Great forest fires, rising oceans and extreme weather occurred and all living things began to die.

As a consequence of the nuclear explosion, Ghandi felt that the East would be entirely destroyed so reluctantly instructed Putin to develop counter weapons. They realised that if they got their people onto Western lands, the weapon would not be able to be used against them because Western humans would be killed too. They therefore formed massive armies and invaded the Western countries. The Western countries, having never faced hostilities before, were unprepared for such a move and capitulated very easily. The forces eventually reached Waterloo in London which was the last great Western stronghold.

By now Putin and Stalin were in a position to use nuclear weapons of their own and laid down an ultimatum to the Western countries to stop forcing their religion upon them. They believed that the West would agree to this and a harmonious peaceful co-existence.

Instead Elvis wore ceremonial attire with valuable jewel-studded symbols and went onto a mass communication device known as the telephone. Elvis sang a fanatical religious song called 'Glory Hallelujah' then commanded the Western forces to detonate hundreds of nuclear weapons to destroy the East. The East was left with no option but to fire back.

The result was the annihilation of the world.

At the end Adam applauded and laughed. "Bravo," he said. "You seriously want me to believe that I am not in a coma when you come up with a story of a nuking killer Elvis haha? Classic. You have blended about two hundred years into one incident. So what happened after the annihilation of the world?"

Alexa smiled beautifully and continued unabashed.

Chapter 10

History of the Future

It took seventy-six nuclear weapons to end the world. That was all. The West fired forty, the East thirty-six. The Prime Minister of Great Britain arranged the first shot. Their name is not recorded in history.

The weapons targeted some the largest cities in the world and billions of humans and animals were killed outright immediately. Even King Elvis was killed whilst using a human waste device called a toilet.

The ways of the old world ended immediately too. Utilities such as power and water ceased. Exchanging something called money for goods and services stopped because it mostly didn't exist, more a fugazi hidden on computers in banks; none of which existed anymore. Elected or forced governments ceased to exist. Armies were mostly destroyed. There were no leaders, no rules, no information, no communication.

The Earth's atmosphere was filled with radiation, smoke and chemicals. The air became unbreathable. Permanent darkness engulfed the planet. The Earth became an instantly hot and hostile world.

The human food chain ceased to operate and became scarce quickly. Humans who lived away from the cities that initially survived the explosions were left to their own devices in horrific conditions. They couldn't breathe. They couldn't eat. The radiation was too great for them. The darkness ensured that they couldn't see to defend themselves. The developing world of equality evaporated into survival of the fittest. Humans attacked and killed each other. Ate each other. Even the fittest couldn't survive. Everyone died within two months.

Everyone that is except for the Preppers.

The Preppers were an elite group of humans who had the foresight and expertise to plan for such a nuclear event. For years in advance they had built bunkers, hoarded food and clean water, dug tunnels and trained to live in a hostile environment. They had built communication systems, formed groups and discussed tactics. Other humans had believed them to be peculiar and ridiculed their every move but the Preppers resisted the cat calls and the humiliation, planned and prepared and planned some more.

Andrew Smith prepared the most. They built a series of tunnels between their bunker and other Preppers, as well as, most importantly, a tunnel to the edge of the underground personnel transport system known as the underground traincar. Smith's innovative thinking finally enabled the few survivors to move reasonable distances and ultimately was the saviour of the human race.

It wasn't that simple though. Smith managed to communicate with other humans via a device known as a CB. There were known to be thousands of Preppers worldwide in both the East and the West, including royalty and world leaders who had amazing facilities. Soon they were all in touch with each other. They made plans to survive. Smith told them of the underground traincar routes and that they should burrow to the edge of them.

Most humans were isolated in their bunkers though and could never tunnel far enough to reach anyone else.

Eventually the power in the CBs died. Eventually the water supplies ran dry and the food ran out. Worse still was that the air in the bunkers quickly became deadly from carbon dioxide regardless of the efforts made to prevent this. Despite the years of preparation, Humans went quiet. A hero named Benny Kristiensen made the brave decision to step outside of their bunker. They died instantly and the incoming air poisoned the remaining survivors in the family killing them all. Preparing for a nuclear event had lengthened life but hadn't saved it.

Smith was different. Smith had protective suits. Many oxygen tanks. Digging equipment. Reference materials. And most important of all: large spaces. Smith's tunnels allowed thirty-six other humans to gather together in his spacious locations. Smith managed to seal some of the underground traincar tunnels.

The thirty-six heralded Smith as Lord Saviour and it was deserved. Their innovation, skill and knowledge was second to none. Smith died aged ninety-six having borne twelve children into a maze of constructed genius with running clean water, an energy supply, food, expansion plans and a complicated time-counting method starting from zero which they called after detonation.

It was now 955 A.D.

Three generations on from Lord Smith, issues began to occur. The radiation from above had made its way through the ground and, whilst health remained good in the community, bearing children became more and more impossible. At first surrogacy was used but it became apparent that humans were not going to survive in this community.

Around 200 A.D. at a time that the population of the Smith community decreased to severely dangerous levels, contact was made with another human community.

The second community, calling themselves the Swales, had developed cloning humans to keep their population levels up. Swales shared the knowledge with Smiths and soon a cloning programme was underway.

Five hundred and sixty-seven years after the detonation, the Smiths and the Swales eventually tunnelled through to each other and the communities engaged.

The advanced genetic engineering of the clones eradicated medical and physical imperfections and eventually perfect humans existed. Paragraph 56 decreed that entropy ensures human deterioration commences aged twenty-five, so the humans were to self destruct at that age having re-cloned themselves first.

Humans had lived a perfect life ever since.

Chapter 11

Questions of Sex

"So you're a clone?" asked Adam.

"Yes," replied Alexa.

"A clone?" he repeated.

"Yes," replied Alexa again.

"Flipping hell," said Adam loudly, and was promptly electrocuted by his suit. "This blood... ooh close." He stopped, realising he was about to swear again. "This thing is really starting to naff me off."

Adam winced and braced himself, realising "naff" might zap him but it fortunately didn't.

"So you're a clone and everyone else is a clone," he continued. "You're all exactly the same."

"Correct."

"Exactly the same?"

"Correct."

"And you don't have children?"

"Correct."

"Can you have children?"

"Pre-adolescent beings not now required," confirmed Alexa.

"But can you?" insisted Adam.

"Decided biological make up of humans does not allow for reproduction," answered Alexa.

"In what sense?"

"No reproductive mechanism."

"You have no ovaries and stuff?"

"No reproductive mechanism."

"So if some hot bloke from the past with er... full reproductive equipment, suddenly cropped up, you'd be able to have sex without any fear of getting pregnant?"

Adam suddenly had an unavoidable grin developing on his face as the idea of sex with the world's most beautiful woman crept into his brain.

"No reproductive mechanism," came the disappointing reply.

Perplexed, Adam tried another simpler question. "Do you have sex?"

"Not understood."

"Sex. Do you have it?"

"Not understood."

"Which bit? Sex or whether you have it?"

"Not have as not understand meaning."

"Wait a minute." An ever elated Adam grinned. "You're telling me that I've come to a place where there's a world full of gorgeous hotties that have yet to be introduced to the joys of the bedroom. So you've got no idea about the... you know... doing it?"

Alexa simply smiled and looked blank.

"You know," continued Adam, "putting the man's..." Adam was electrocuted by the suit.

"Ayaz," he shrieked. "Well this is unfair. How the he... er, how do I explain this one without using... you know... the M and the W?"

Alexa smiled without reacting.

"Basics," said Adam refusing to let the topic and perhaps a wonderful opportunity go by. "So the hee hee goes into the nah nah and it's all very nice."

Nothing from Alexa.

"Penis? Vagina?" queried Adam whilst bracing himself for a possible shock that never came.

Alexa stared blankly.

Adam pointed to his lower region and then Alexa's. "No? Aw we need an anatomy lesson. Remove the suit and I'll show you," he said with a wink.

Alexa walked from the room leaving Adam guiltily

feeling he had gone a step too far and embarrassed the poor girl. He also regretted failing to ask any questions on the other nine million topics that he was burning to get answers for.

Seconds later, Alexa walked into the room, entirely naked. At first Adam's heart skipped a beat with glee at the prospect of this naked beautiful woman but then it nearly stopped beating full stop.

Alexa was no woman. Nor man. Their legs met at the bottom of the torso and there was nothing but a continuation of smooth skin. They had no breasts or nipples. No navel. Alexa was human shaped but by no means human.

Chapter 12

Questions of Suits and Waste

Adam stared in shock and awe at the naked Alexa and though he wanted to, much like when witnessing a road traffic accident, he could not look away.

"Anatomy lesson required?" asked Alexa patiently four times before acquiring any sort of a response from Adam.

"Er no. I've got it," murmured a bashful and somewhat sexually confused Adam.

Alexa left and returned a short time later wearing the electrocuting suit again. "Any more questions?"

"How do you remove this horrific suit?" was first to Adam's mind.

"Suit programmed self remove when cleaning, repair, injury, education," Alexa instructed.

"So if I take a bath or have a bad knee, the suit comes off by itself?" asked Adam already planning never to put it back on again.

"Correct," came the reply.

"So why does anyone even wear them?" he asked.

"Compulsory."

"But you can't be electrocuted if you're not wearing it. Come on Alexa. Ditch the suit and put on an Adidas tracky. You'll feel good, believe me."

"Impossible. Compulsory," Alexa replied.

"Why?" persisted Adam. "Does some massive fly come and spew your face off if you're not wearing one?"

"Immediate lockdown chamber. Oxygen eradicated. Termination," came the sinister reply.

"F… oooh. It all seems a bit extreme. You lot live by some seriously severe rules. So you all live in tunnels.

Can't swear or shout or scream or argue. You don't have sex. You can't even mention a gender or religion without being fried. You have to die aged twenty-five and you even make your replacement before you go. Nice. How old is a new clone?"

"Human body age twenty-three years after conception," replied Alexa.

"Two years!" Adam almost shrieked before correcting himself to avoid being zapped. "Two years is not enough. That's not a life. Good grief. Who decided two years was a good idea? I know some sixty-year-olds who are fit as fiddles. Ho wait! How do you go to the toilet? You have no… bits."

"Committee decide rules," responded Alexa. "Toilet not required. No waste."

"Eh? You don't use a toilet because you have no waste?"

"Anatomy lesson required?" asked Alexa.

"God no," replied Adam, followed by a sharp electrocution to his body. When he regained his composure he calmly asked, "How do you have no waste?"

"Exact nutritional quantities," Alexa replied.

"Oh no," moaned Adam. "You're going to tell me you don't eat aren't you. Steak sandwich? Beer? Chocolate? Oh no. This place is a nightmare. I knew this was going to happen. I blame Darren and Annabelle with all their vegan nonsense. No nice food. It was always going to happen. So what do you eat? Tofu on rye crisps or something equally unpleasant no doubt?"

Alexa showed Adam a small green bar about the size of a fun-size Mars Bar. It looked about as appetising as a green bar might and Adam screwed up his nose. "I just know that's going to taste chronic and then bung me right up," he groaned. "So no eating. No cooking. No even going for a right good poo?"

"Exact nutrients. No waste," confirmed Alexa.

With his head in his hands Adam moaned. This place was a nightmare. "So what do you do for fun?"

"Arbeit," came the reply.

Adam's eyes widened again. "Nazis!" he whispered. He was in a world that represented a futuristic concentration camp. "So you work for two years and then you die. That's no life. Who's in charge?"

"No 'in charge'. Everyone equal."

"Believe me, honey. Er, I mean chummy. Whatever you are. Someone will be more equal than everyone else. Who is in this committee?"

"Unknown."

"Exactly!" triumphed Adam. "It'll be like the Soviet Union mark my words. Take me to them please."

"Committee not approached," explained Alexa.

"I'm a real-life human and where I come from we have rights, sweetheart, er, mate. I'd appreciate it if you would find out if we can see them. They will surely be interested in seeing me. I have testicles remember. Everyone loves to see those bad boys."

As Alexa left the room, Adam was recovering from his electric shock for using the word boys.

Chapter 13

The Committee

It took an age for Alexa to return and Adam had used the time to plot every conceivable way to escape from this modern world prison.

He figured that this breed of futuristic humans who had no fun and were not even allowed to yell or swear were likely to be soft as crap in a fist fight, so he settled upon knocking the teeth out of every perfectly smiling Alexa he came across and simply walking out of the place as his best idea.

Being a man of restraint and reason, though, he remained calm and allowed the opportunity for a less violent approach.

Alexa eventually returned and passed him onto six more Alexas who had been instructed to transport him to the committee. He strangely felt a touch of sadness as he said bye to what he had come to think of as his Alexa although, within a minute or so, the others had acted, behaved and spoken exactly the same and it felt like his Alexa was still with him.

He walked through an incredible maze of underground corridors, each one feeding a series of others. They were all the same, as was everyone they passed. Everyone was busy. There was no laughter. No singing. No fun.

After walking to near exhaustion they stopped in a room which looked exactly the same as the one he had left but with more beds. He was hungry but felt like he had a horrendous bout of constipation and his mouth was dry and felt like he had been licking a sandy beach.

He was handed one of the fun-sized bars. "Why thank you," he said sarcastically. "I will feast on this like Louis

XIV."

Holding the tiny green bar in his hand, Adam eyed it suspiciously like it might kill him. He sniffed it and it smelled like fermented cabbage which made him a) regret sniffing it and b) heave. Holding his nose he shoved the whole thing into his mouth. It reminded him of the time he had been at school and his friends had pinned him down before Fatty McEwan farted into his face. The taste was certainly similar. He chewed. And chewed, And chewed some more. Then chewed some more.

"Tasty," he spluttered through the chewing whist trying not to throw up.

Once he'd managed to swallow the thing, Adam felt remarkably well. He was refreshed, his mouth dryness gone, and even though his sarcastic request for a cup of tea was met with blank smiles by the Alexas, he truly didn't need a drink in any case.

They retired to the beds and Adam slept like a log. After ten hours or so he awoke to find the Alexas were all still sleeping. About ninety minutes later at exactly at the same time, the Alexas woke and rose. Adam was later informed that eleven hours and thirty-seven minutes was the optimum recovery and bodily repair amount of sleep needed for a human, and he remembered a time when he was a shift worker and got about three hours maximum.

Another day of tunnel walking and another incredible night of sleep was incredibly boring. There was literally nothing of any excitement in this place. Forcing his bar down made him long for a greasy cheesy burger. He'd raised the question of whether the Alexas were aware of motorised transport. They were, it seemed, but then he was lectured on how the human body functioned and how walking was the best form of muscle manipulation.

Replying that he didn't give a toss and he just wanted a lift had only caused him to be electrocuted.

Adam did utilise the lengthy walking time to good effect. He asked question after question of the future he found himself in, including the known history of how it had come to be the way it was.

He concluded that a combination of good intention, attempts at equality, kindness to each other and above all, necessity, had manifested into a horrendous world where there was no individuality, the strictest of rules and punishment and absolutely nothing to live for.

Living in the future had become a literal death sentence.

On the third day, Adam was left in an empty room alone whilst the Alexas went off to arrange his meeting with the committee. He stood, because seating was not something that existed here and felt remarkably nervous. His brain was visualising finding Mikhail Gorbachev, Lenin and the pig out of *Animal Farm* sitting there in military uniform and feared that he would be sentenced to years of hard labour for being different.

The committee actually couldn't have been more different to that. They were in fact twelve Alexas, identical in every way to the previous Alexas. They were pleasant, open to conversation and in no way fearsome. They welcomed Adam warmly and explained that they wished to examine every possible piece of information from the past that he held and, furthermore, would do anything they could to establish how he had come to be here and why.

For sixteen days, Adam regaled tales of the past. At first he revelled in the limelight but as the clarification questions intensified he was alarmed at his actual lack of detailed knowledge and wished he'd paid a little more attention in history or had actually bothered to read a book in his adult life.

Regardless, the committee hung on his every word

whilst a team of secretary Alexas made copious notes. It was explained to Adam that barely any historical artefacts, transcripts or records had been preserved after detonation. The circumstances meant that there was simply no space to keep unessential items, no power meant anything not recorded on paper was essentially lost and much more importance was given to scientific details to enable survival. History had mostly been passed from generation to generation before people started writing it down again. Whilst the committee had absolutely no idea how Adam could have come from the past and to some degree did not even believe he had, there was no getting away from the solid fact that he had testicles and the anatomy of a historical human. This fact, they thought, warranted some credibility to Adam's story.

Ironing out the differences between Hitler, Napoleon and definitely Elvis Presley caused the most consternation. Quite simply the committee did not believe that Elvis was only an entertainer. For a start, these people had never experienced entertainment and had no idea what was meant by singing, dancing, and hip swinging let alone 'uhuha'. Adam's rendition of 'Suspicious Minds' with full fist-pumping dance routine did little to convince anyone about anything.

The committee were adamant that Elvis was the most powerful King of Europa and that Adam was mistaken. Elvis's actions in the great nuclear war had been debated for centuries. Some considered Elvis to be a great leader, the greatest of all, and in fact a small group had left the facility thirty years ago insisting that they were leaving to follow the example of the King.

Adam enquired what happened to them to be told it was unknown but it was expected that, given they went to the over world, they must be dead. This prompted Adam to tell the committee all about the outside world. He covered the beautiful landscape, the trees, the fruit, the wonderful oxygen-rich air and the blissful warmth. He covered the massive dogs, spiders, flies and the normal-sized crocodiles. He talked about being attacked by a giant aggressive crow, the killer seagulls and the fluffy cute things.

The committee was suspicious of Adam's description of the outside. No one had even tried stepping outside since Benny Kristiensen except for the Elvis fanatics. They pointed out that Adam had arrived unconscious. Adam raised that in opening the door, the air would have poisoned anyone if it was poisonous. Disappointingly for that argument, the committee explained an intricate airlock and filtering system that was in place for just such an occasion in which Adam had entered. Adam's argument that it was probably this airlock that had made him go unconscious fell on deaf ears as did him pointing out that if light was escaping, it was not airtight. They were very proud of their systems and disagreed wholeheartedly that anything critical could be thought of them.

Adam spent probably too long a time pointing out and arguing the insanity of spending time and effort on an intricate door system to the outside world if there was never a possibility that someone would use it. The committee pointed out that they had used it with Adam and therefore it was justified despite Adam countering that the possibility of a random naked bloke turning up from the past was nothing short of ridiculous. The committee were always smiling and unflappable and always fell back on the argument that this series of events did happen and there was no getting away from that.

They theorised the giant animals. It was known that at the time of the detonations dogs were the most popular pet and therefore there were millions of them worldwide.

If, though it was unlikely, some survived, then it was likely the biggest, best hunters would thrive and breed with other large dogs. If food had become plentiful and oxygen good as Adam claimed, then growth would accelerate. The same could be said of birds and insects and if little furry things existed as a food supply then it was expected they must breed a lot. If humans had managed to survive, then why not other animals?

Adam suddenly realised that crocodiles had survived the extinction of the dinosaurs and therefore would survive anything. He was concerned at the blank expressions of the committee before realising that they had absolutely no concept of a dinosaur whatsoever. This led to a whole new lengthy conversation about the prehistoric world which was mostly met with astonishment and a touch of disbelief from the committee. That Adam was basing most of his knowledge of dinosaurs on the film *Jurassic Park* probably wasn't helping his new persona as a palaeontologist.

By day seventeen Adam had covered a multitude of historical issues.

These included:

World Wars One and Two which clarified the gift of pearls issue to the surprise of the committee. At least Adam thought they were surprised, because they never expressed any emotion whatsoever. The horrors of Hitler's actions which were simply outside of the comprehension of their society were met without any emotion or anything other than questions of fact.

Captain Cook, Drake and other explorers including accidentally calling Columbus Columbo throughout, which made him laugh when he thought about the historical consequences of humans believing a scruffy little detective with a glass eye had been responsible for finding the Americas.

The Romans and ancient Greeks, or in reality an account of the films *Gladiator*, *Spartacus* and *Jason and the Argonauts*. Adam had kept a copy of the *Iliad* by Homer on a coffee table for about five years that had been his wife's. He left it there because he felt it made visitors think he was intellectual and he had attempted to read it in school so felt justified. In actual fact he had struggled with pronouncing the names Agamemnon and Menelaus and actually had no idea what it was really about.

Slavery. In a deliberate attempt to whitewash the British role in the horrific enslaving of innocents, Adam blamed the entire episode on the United States of America. His Civil War and War of Independence lessons were surely muddled together but in fairness they were better than his attempt at explaining his own country's civil war or the revolutions in France and Russia.

Vietnam, Cold War, Boer War, Napoleonic Wars, Genghis Khan, The Falklands, Iraq, 9/11 and Margaret Thatcher. These topics made Adam realise he was telling a constant historical tale of terror and humans killing, or causing abject misery to other humans.

Transport. In a deliberate change of tactics to get away from death and destruction, Adam described the planes, trains and automobiles that had once enabled humans to travel the world. He told stories of flying through the clouds. However, he very soon found himself on the Titanic disaster, the Great Train Robbery, tanks and spitfires, 9/11 again and how the car had choked the atmosphere and began the demise of animals and insects. Try as he might he could not stay clear of mankind's ability to kill itself and everything else.

Film and Television. Initially starting by describing

Tarantino classics and the 1960s spaghetti westerns, Adam realised they were all movies that glorified killing human beings. Try as he might he couldn't think of a movie that held his generation in a good light so he quickly turned to television and *Seinfeld*. In trying to describe what a show about nothing entailed he laughed when he realised he was almost word for word recreating an episode. "I think I can sum up the show with one word. Nothing," he said. "Nothing. What does that mean?" they asked. "The show is about nothing," he said. "Well it must be about something. Even nothing is something," they said, prompting hilarity from Adam that simply was not understood by his audience.

Popular music. This went better and he explained Beatlemania was not an all-conquering army. He covered Bowie, The Stones, Oasis, Pavarotti and Billy Joel. Adam's rendition of 'Piano Man' was significantly better than his 'Nessun Dorma' and he was secretly quite proud of his Mick Jagger impression.

Adam talked everything from his world and the past of his world. He laughed. He sang. He danced. When he talked of Darren and his wife he cried. There was never any reaction from the committee. They were designed not to have one. By the end he was exhausted of information. The overriding question that the committee asked was "Why?" Why play football or tennis or run or ride a bicycle. Why visit a part of the world or cook a nice meal? Why get drunk and make an idiot of yourself?

Why? Why? Why?

The answer was always the same. "For fun," said Adam.

It was a concept they did not understand.

Chapter 14

Fun

Adam decided that if he was destined to spend the rest of his life in this pleasureless purgatory, he needed to make some changes. Fun was number one on his agenda.

The committee seemed to be an open, honest bunch and to a degree hailed Adam as some kind of sensation. Providing he stuck to the draconian rules on everything, he might just be able to introduce some entertainment into their bleak world.

Adam decided to host a sing-song. He spent a painful morning teaching the committee the words to 'Hey Jude'. Time and again they interrupted him to ask what was meant by the lyrics. "Let her into your heart." "What mean? Surgery required?" asked one. This led to a two hour discussion on what love was.

Trying to explain love to emotionless, nonsexual, nonbinary beings proved to be difficult to the point where Adam yelled in despair and frustration and was promptly electrocuted. In a change of tack, he then spent considerable time pleading with the committee to de-electrocute the suit.

The committee explained that the decision to implement an instant punishment method had been made by Lord Smith after an unruly blaggard named John Preston had stolen vital community provisions and blamed his indiscretion on an innocent bystander. Smith could not tolerate crime or misbehaviour. In fairness, everyone else's lives depended upon togetherness and collective harmony.

Preston was put to death by being thrown into the pit. The pit was a giant deep hole where waste and the dead were deposited. It was a most horrific way to die. It was expected that if Preston had survived the fall, and he might well have done given the soft nature of the contents of the pit, he would have slowly drowned or worse, starved to death, ravaged with disease.

Preston was the first to go this way. More were to follow. Lord Smith saw it that arguments, fights and even illness could not be tolerated because the survival of the human race depended entirely upon being able to get along and stay healthy. The death penalty bar was set desperately low because Smith felt it had to be.

As time improved technology, the suit was invented. By then Smith was long gone, but a representative committee of the people decreed the suit would be worn by all as they felt it would prevent any indiscretion which would lead to the death penalty. Since the advent of the first suit three hundred years ago, no human had been put to death for civil disobedience.

"Civil disobedience!" yelped Adam which led to an instant shock which felled him to the floor. He took a moment to recover before calmly repeating "Civil disobedience. You've got to be kidding. I can appreciate that in the early days you might have needed some strict rules. I've seen *The Walking Dead*. There's always one lunatic who wanders off and gets half of the others eaten so I get it. But now? All these years later? You're all the same. You all think the same and feel the same. If you feel anything at all that is, and I'm not sure about that. I'll bet no one ever even considered doing anything wrong. So the only person being punished is me."

"Forty-seven times," said one of the committee.

"Exactly," replied Adam. "I'm no threat. I'm a good guy, yet I'm like a piece of overcooked KFC here. So I swear a bit or shout a bit or use the wrong pronoun. So what? Who decided that all of these things should deserve a blast anyway?"

That rhetorical question led to a thirty-eight-minute explanation of the history of the decision-making towards suit punishments. Adam was bored half to death by it. It reminded him of Darren blaring on about being offended by this, that and the other. When the lecture eventually finished Adam said:

"So 'Hey Jude'…"

By mid-afternoon the committee was somewhat harmonising "nah nah nah nah nah nah nah, hey Jude," whilst Adam sang the main tune. It was brutal. It reminded Adam of being at school while the crazy music teacher would get annoyed and yell at the kids during assembly for mumbling the songs in a tuneless unenthusiastic fashion. It was clear that 'Adam and the Alexas' were not going to be number one on *Top of the Pops* 955 A.D.

The good news was that the Alexas did not get bored. It was an emotion that had been removed in the cloning modification process. The committee considered that what Adam was doing was education and education formed a major part of their arbeit so at least they were game for Adam's impoverished efforts. In a final and somewhat terrible rendition, Adam broke into the Paul McCartney "Judey, Judey" screaming part and was promptly electrocuted by the suit.

That was enough to put an end to that and, instead, the first underground championship cricket test match was created.

Using a ball of elastic bands and wooden table legs as bat and wickets, the construction of which had caused Adam to be electrocuted for damaging the table, Adam launched his best googly at committee batsman number one. It had been a while since he bowled and his googly became a yorker and headed directly for the batsman's head. It struck them just under the chin before obliterating the wicket.

"Howzat!" screamed Adam with arms wide open to an imaginary umpire. The electricity that then rippled through his body was so intense it floored him and rendered him unconscious for a moment.

He woke in intense pain and looked questioningly at the committee batsman who was standing over him smiling beautifully.

"Shouting. Assault," they said.

Adam groaned. If accidentally hitting someone with a ball was assault then sport was definitely out. His world heavyweight boxing idea was in tatters.

Music and sport were his go-to fun creators and both were ruled out in this godforsaken place.

Adam had once shared a love of the great outdoors with his wife. Long before she had become ill and way before Darren had been born, Adam had explored some of the world's great locations with her but this passion had perished with the demise of his loved one. She had once crawled around the top of the leaning tower of Pisa because she was scared of the height and the uneven camber, even though there was a giant fence that meant she couldn't possibly have fallen out. He loved her so incredibly much for having even braved the stairs to be up there with him.

They loved to watch the sea and sat for hours on beaches, barbequing steaks on the sand, regardless of the weather. They walked over hill and meadow, mountain and road. Always hand in hand and always chatting. Rivers had been rowed. Seas had been swum. Forests had been foraged.

When she started to falter for breath and energy, their passion became impossible and by the time the worst had happened they were virtual recluses. Partaking in sport was his only reason to venture out now. For years, Adam's outdoor world had lost its joy but being forced underground in this world without fun had stirred the passion again. Adam found a determination to find joy in the outdoors again.

Convincing the committee that the second someone stepped outside, their lungs wouldn't turn to stone proved difficult. Adam argued that he had spent ages outside before he found them and he was perfectly alright. The health reports produced by the committee argued otherwise. He wasn't in perfect shape.

"Yes but I'm nearly twenty years older than what you have decreed should be dead so I think I'm doing pretty well," countered Adam, "and I've never felt better than when I was in the air out there. There are animals and food. Beautiful fruit. Believe me it's better than eating the fun-sized crud bar. Let me go out. I'll spend a bit of time out there and then you can test me to your heart's content. Believe me. It'll be worth it."

Pleading to the emotions of an emotionless being was always going to be a tough gig but Adam, if nothing else, was persistent in his arguments, the best one being that he had been outside and was still alive. It was hard to argue against that but the committee was steadfast in its refusal to break a near thousand-year-old rule to remain underground.

In a spark of brilliance Adam came up with the education argument. Alexa had inferred that they were obliged to seek education where possible. "What could be more educational than exploring a whole world – boom!" said he. The boom and accompanying imaginary mic drop was probably an unnecessary addition by Adam but having banged on and on and on without any breakthrough, it felt like a pivotal moment.

It was. The committee began to consider their options.

They checked their skin's ability to withstand the sun's radiation. They checked their breathing function. They did tests on their eyes in which Adam had no idea what was going on though he nearly fainted when he watched something long and metal-looking being shoved into the eye of a smiling Alexa.

Amazingly, they agreed and two days later Adam led an educational party of cloned humans to leave the safety of their underground catacombs for the first time in nine hundred and fifty-five years.

Chapter 15

Outside

Adam watched his companion team of intrepid explorers closely as they braced themselves for the unknown. They were emotionally modified not to feel fear and yet their automatic responses to danger were most definitely present and left them acting very peculiarly as hormones and adrenalin did their jobs.

They only walked for an hour or so to an exit point. It was different to where he came in. He was informed this door to the outside did not involve the lengthy walk through the darkness and he was definitely grateful for that. Plundering his way through a pitch-dark tunnel with a load of grinning Alexas might have been a hardship too far.

A large metal tunnel block with a small door the same as the one he had seen before stood between them and the outside world. The small door opened and he walked through first, disappointingly finding himself in the darkness of a tunnel. Confused he asked why and was informed it was an air seal to prevent poisonous gases entering the main chambers. He was about to ask what the point of that was if he had been able to simply walk in from the outside at the previous door he entered when an Alexa informed him that in his darkened scramble, he had somehow breached a similar air lock door. This had caused significant consternation among the Smith/Swales population who had instigated large-scale evacuation preparation. It was not known how the seal had been breached.

Adam apologised for any inconvenience he had caused but chuckled to himself at his little influence of carnage to these people who lacked any excitement whatsoever.

A shuffle through the darkness led to another sealed door and a clunk, a click and a ping in the darkness before a creaky opening and the radiant heat and brightness of outside blessing Adam's face.

He stepped into the brilliant daylight and rubbed frantically at his eyes until they no longer felt like they were going to be seared from his skull. He breathed the fresh air, so different from the manufactured oxygen of the tunnels. It ripped into his lungs and he immediately felt strong and good. He smiled. It felt good to be on Mother Earth's surface.

Adam turned to the group of lookalikes cowering in the entrance to the tunnels. "I thought you lot were supposed to have no fear," he teased.

"Danger always avoided where possible." A responder smiled.

"It's fine, come on," reassured Adam, nervously looking around for killer dogs.

The team of explorers set foot from the safety of their tunnel and marched to where Adam stood. For a very alarming minute, all of them coughed and spluttered for breath, clawed at their stinging eyes and fell to their knees whilst Adam stood horrified, hoping and praying that they would be ok.

They were and recovered quickly from the culture shock of the different atmosphere.

"Thank God," said Adam as the first one returned to their feet and beamed a perfect smile at him.

Adam stopped and looked at himself in amazement.

He had not been electrocuted for his God comment.

"God," he said again. Nothing.

"God," he screamed at the top of his voice. Nothing.

"Jesus crapping God tits arsehole bastard," yelled

Adam with no suit response.

"Yessssss! The suit doesn't work out here," he elatedly yelled at the group.

Human clones of the year 955 A.D. had never previously seen a middle-aged man dance around like he was bopping to the beat of 1990s Ibiza trance but they did in that moment. This was closely followed by a full rendition of 'I Want to Break Free' by Queen with imaginary hoover and high heels.

When he was done, he was out of breath, sweating and feeling horrendous. The fun bars did not cater for overexuberance. He had lost essential salts and liquid that simply had not been provided for him. Immediately spying a large open leaf that was covered in morning dew, he snapped it from the tree where it grew. The Alexa party collectively gasped. They had never seen anyone damage a plant before. Adam folded the plant and drank the dew water. He grinned at them, saying, "Perfect."

It became apparent that the group had no idea where their bars of goodness came from because when Adam argued that leaves must be taken from growing plants to make them, they were insistent that this could not be the case as destruction of anything was forbidden and led to an early trip to the pit.

"This pit is a form of destruction," said Adam. "Your whole world is a contradiction. You're free to do anything but not allowed to anything. You're not allowed to pull a leaf but you can make a plant and God knows what into a bar. You can't destroy a leaf but you have to... have to destroy yourselves after two years of life. What do you do? Throw yourself into this grotty pit of doom? Horrendous."

"Yes," came the shocking response from one of the Alexas.

"What the actual?" announced Adam. "This pit is either massive or full. There must be thousands of you down there."

It was massive. The entrance was only six feet wide but it led into a tunnel that then led to a cavern that was deeper and further than anyone knew. It was the perfect safe disposal system. No trace of anything. Alexas stepped into the breach on their second birthday and... bosh. Gone for good.

None of these emotionless, anti-humans had ever given a thought to the agonising pain and suffering that must occur once entry into that pit commenced.

Adam wagged an aggressive finger at the group. "Not for the first time around here, you lot have been so far from frigging human that it defies belief," he growled. "Come on. You have some education to do. This is grass. This is the sky. This is a tree."

Exactly seventeen minutes and thirty-three seconds after entering the natural world again, and he knew this because he was told so in the subsequent hearing, Adam said, "This is an orange. It's an edible fruit." Followed very quickly by, "These are a shedload of massive midges. Run!"

Chapter 16

Sad

"Seventeen minutes thirty-three seconds after arrival attacked insects. Bitten. Multiple. Adam egomaniacal," said an Alexa that had huge yellow and red lumps filled with pus all over their face.

The auto-immune systems of the clones had gone berserk. They had never experienced anything of the kind and quite simply their bodies had gone into overdrive wondering how to deal with such an atrocity.

"4323 remained above," continued the bitten Alexa, "unfound."

After his initial run to safety, Adam had turned in horror to see the group of Alexas standing in the swarm of midges and not reacting in any way as the insects crawled over them and clearly bit them.

He looked around and snapped a large palm-leafed branch from a tree and quickly returned swishing the branch to clear the midges. One swish walloped the Alexa he now knew as 4323 in the face knocking them to the ground in a heap.

Adam grabbed the Alexa nearest to him and dragged them in the direction of the tunnel shouting, "Come this way." The Alexa had never been forcibly touched before and reacted by lifting Adam from the floor and throwing him twenty feet into the long grass.

He learned his lesson quickly but the method of individually and politely requesting each and every Alexa accompany him to safety proved a terrible method of dealing with a midge swarm attack. Big midges at that! By the time he had managed to recover everyone to safety he had received three massive bites himself. One was to the eyelid which immediately hampered his ability to see what he was doing.

In the brouhaha he had failed to notice 4323 slumped in the long grass. The discovery of their absence prompted Adam to return above ground – alone because there was no way he was ever getting the committee to allow another exploration party. He searched and searched but 4323 was never to be found.

Now, with an unbearable itching to his head and a yellow liquid pus running from his eye to his chin, Adam stood in front of the committee facing trial for the offences of destruction of a fellow comrade and endangering the safety of the population.

Interrupting and pointing out that 'comrade' was very communisty and would freak out any Americans that they might come across had only served to produce the welcoming smile that was always on offer from the Alexas and then a lengthy lecture on the severity of the situation and the history of the law.

Until now it hadn't occurred to Adam that he could be remotely blamed for the loss of 4323 or the injury to the others. Ok, he might have predicted an attack of some sort of insect or animal but he had warned the committee of the spiders and dogs and suchlike yet they had agreed to the education party. It was his apparent attempt to save his own skin which was the major consternation.

Adam's saviour was his palm-flapping actions despite the accident that had left an Alexa missing.

"You not sentenced destruction pit because life-saving actions," said one of the committee as they passed judgement. "One year isolation. Arbeit 12.23."

Adam sat shocked. These hypocritical fake humans had considered throwing him into a pit of dead people because some of their mates had been bitten by some midges. It certainly wasn't his fault that one had gone missing, in his opinion, regardless that he had whacked them in the first place.

He became outraged and considered what was said. One year of isolation with all but the designated sleep time as work. This wouldn't do at all.

"Now see here," said Adam speaking as officiously as he could without raising his voice, "I will not be isolated. It is my intention to come and go as I please, including outside."

The electricity caught him by surprise and he fell to the floor with a yelp. "Disobedience," was the last voice he heard as a door slammed leaving him alone.

It was as though a sudden wave of emotions swept over Adam as the realisation that he was not going home to his normal world hit him.

In his quest for survival and then the excitement of the Alexas, electric suits, stories of the future and everything else, Adam simply hadn't taken the time to reflect on what he had left behind. He hadn't really believed he had left anything behind, such was his steadfast certainty that he would return there.

The one-year sentence had somehow put a sense of finality on his ongoing adventure and now he sat on the floor of an empty room, deep under a futuristic forested London town, alone with his thoughts.

Grief at the loss of Darren and Annabelle consumed him. They had been killed in a nuclear war caused by the greed of powerful people. His only son had been taken from him. He prayed to God and Jesus Christ that they had been taken quickly and not had to endure the post apocalyptic nightmare that must have existed for a while.

Adam sobbed and cried. He thought of the beautiful girl next door and his wife and his own parents and sobbed some more.

The friends he made in his days at war came to mind.

His friends of days gone by who shared evening meals and wine with his wife on couples' dates. His work colleagues. His sports team. Everything and everyone was gone. He cried for them and he cried for him. A sole survivor left in a world and a place where he did not fit.

It was the first of many a long and painful night of loneliness and sorrow. He barely slept. There was no longer a splendid comfy bed provided for him. He slept on the floor if he slept at all.

Arbeit was better. It kept him occupied. He was put to work in a vast and incredible underground cavern that was once a large station perhaps. The cavern housed plants. They looked like a cross between a cabbage and tomato if such a thing could be envisaged. They were made of red fleshy fruit but in the shape of cabbage leaves. Thousands upon thousands of them in row after row grew steadily and quickly in a fine sandy black soil. He tended them but it was easy. Weeds did not grow and there were no slugs or pests to contend with. Once fully grown, they were picked and placed into a large metal funnel situated at the wall face of the cavern where they disappeared. Seeds were then brought to him and he planted more. Once every ten crops, the soil was replaced with new by shovelling it into another funnel in what was backbreaking work. New soil was always there the next day. He didn't ask questions of what happened to the plants as he presumed they were processed into the disgusting bars, nor where the seeds or soil came from. No one spoke to him and he did not speak back.

Adam worked all day and he cried all night.

After weeks he could take no more. Instead of working, he sat by the cabbatos as he liked to call them, and did nothing. At first the other Alexas paid no attention to him or did not notice but after a while they shot him curious glances adorned with beautiful smiles and sure enough, a short time after that, the suit blasted him with electricity. He coiled in pain but simply allowed himself to lie in the soil.

Shock after shock thrashed his body but still Adam lay unmoved. He decided that the electricity would stop his heart soon enough and that was good enough for him. Instead, the pain became more and more bearable and whilst the shocks were more powerful, his pain tolerance became stronger. Regardless he lay motionless. Eventually the suit stopped shocking him.

This generation didn't understand Adam. They didn't understand his emotions or his grief. They did not possess the ability to have longing for home like he had. Furthermore they did not comprehend stubbornness or resolve and had never envisaged that someone would embrace pain like he had. The behaviour of this man had always been a concern to be managed to them. Now, on seeing his ability to defy all the rules and equally manipulate his body to defy the punishment, they did not know what do to. It was decided they should simply dispose of him in the pit and proceedings to write a law to be able to enable that to happen were just underway when, after four days of lying in the mud, Adam sat up. He was hungry. Really hungry.

He wolfed down two full cabbatos. They should have been picked and were overripe and a little sludgy in places. It mattered not. They tasted amazing and for the first time in as long as he could remember he smiled. Adam found the water supply and drank thirstily from the metal pipe that fed the pure underground water to the plants.

He stopped and pulled at the pipe revealing more from the rock wall. It was made from copper. Adam thought and then he smiled. In fact he laughed out loud and with a somewhat deranged look on his face set about his latest project.

Chapter 17

Booze

Adam loved a glass of Montepulciano D'abruzzo, preferably with a rare fillet steak, some button mushrooms and a hearty mound of skin off, beef dripping in an old sticky pan with black bits in it, cooked chips. Chips. Not French fries or skinny fries or chunky wedges, twice cooked, thrice cooked, unpeeled or any other pretentious nonsense that had been invented. Proper old-fashioned chips, washed down with some Tuscan magnificence.

His mouth watered at the prospect but cabbatos was all he had and they would have to do. He gathered many of the neglected plants and placed them into a container used for fetching water before removing his admittedly supremely comfortable Nike and Adidas boot and squidging his bare foot into the fleshy leaves of the plant. The cabbatos mashed down beautifully into an almost black watery paste. He added more plants and squashed again. Soon he was able to pour the black liquid into a separate container and when the container was nearly full, he topped it with water before leaving it under a loose lid. He would have moved heaven and Earth for a bag of brewer's yeast but he was hopeful and, in that hope, had found in himself a new lease of life.

His night-time fun bar made him feel well and he urinated for the first time in forever. Sadly this was into the corner of his room such was the lack of a toilet but he fell asleep somewhat content and then slept well with not one tear or sob.

The next day, he worked hard in his cabbato field and even whistled 'Whistle While You Work' while he worked. The pitch of his whistle made the nearest Alexa involuntarily jump and Adam laughed at the spectacle and wished he could shout "boo" at one every now and then without being electrocuted.

After three days he checked his liquid. A few bubbles and a slight foam had started to form. He punched the air in delight and sealed the container with a lid.

Having cobbled together a still by coiling some of the copper pipe between two containers, Adam's heart suddenly sank. He had never noticed fire, an oven or a group of Alexas huddling around a bike shed sharing a cigarette. He suddenly realised heating his liquid might prove to be a problem.

It was. Whilst electricity was in abundance, heating appliances did not appear to have been re-invented yet.

Adam thought hard. "The Library of Historical Artefacts!" he exclaimed.

As audacious as his plan was, it was the only plan he could think of. He felt sure that being found stealing any historical artefacts meant being thrown into the pit faster than you could say sorry, meaning that was out of the question, so he had to go with a potentially much more painful and dangerous option.

For a few weeks he worked hard in the cabbatos field although pacing up and down past his home brew became his obsession. He had no idea when it was ready but one day he took a chance.

"Alexa," he called to someone nearby, "I've had an idea about the artefacts library. I don't know why we didn't do this before but I can name and explain all of the items in there. For education. Education do you hear?"

Adam then said the word "education" about three hundred times just to ensure his message was getting across.

The committee loved the idea and soon he was on his

way to the library. The walk was torturously long because Adam knew he had to do it in reverse under less relaxed conditions but in actual fact it was not far and Adam soon found himself in the grandly titled Library of Historical Artefacts. The Library of Historical Artefacts was in fact a very large room with super high ceilings and was smoothly painted white, with dim lighting and a fusty smell. It was shelved out with eight large rustic wooden shelves built on each of the four walls. The shelves were at least three inches thick, ready to take the weight of the artefacts. In actual fact it was a room with very few items in it. There were certainly more shelves than items, as if it had been anticipated that they would be filled, only for the archaeologists to fail to come up with anything.

Between the grand and empty shelves immediately opposite hung three pictures on the wall. The first was a picture of Kevin De Bruyne in his Manchester City kit, holding aloft the World Cup, under a cloud of pale blue and white ticker tape. Underneath it said 'Belgium to win Qatar'. The rest was ripped away. It looked like a magazine picture and had clearly been badly Photoshopped. The blurring colours around the edges revealed it had clearly previously been the Premier League trophy before the implementation of the World Cup into the picture.

"If only whoever Photoshopped that could have known the implications on history a thousand years later," said Adam to no one in particular, though no one in particular had any idea what he was on about in any case so it didn't matter.

Next to the footballer was a poster stating 'Look what you gain when you travel by train. InterCity 125 makes the going easy.' There were four InterCity black and yellow trains depicted with times to places from Reading. "I remember these," reminisced Adam. "Was it bollocks a smooth fifty-one minutes from Reading to Bath mind." Adam winced when he realised he had sworn. There was no electric shock. "Woah, that must be a word that they don't know about?" He pondered and smiled, knowing he would use it every other word from now on.

The third picture was an enamel female toilet sign. It was rusted and the corner was missing. Adam pointed at it. "Now this was a door sign to a toilet for a gender that isn't me. Just before the war, these started to disappear and communal toilets were popping up all over the place. This was entirely problematic because the me... I mean the gender the same as me were, shall we say, somewhat messy when they went and they would also leave the seats up which really annoyed the girls." Zap. "Damn," said Adam as he collapsed to his knees with the shock. Zap went the suit again which folded him over. "Not fair. I was trying so hard and doing so well. There should be a removal of the rules during education."

An examination of the shelves revealed some interesting items. There was a black Dell laptop with a cracked screen and no power cable. Adam explained what it did when it worked but was powerless to demonstrate anything worthwhile.

There was a maroon Maglite torch, missing a bulb and with corroded battery rust all over the handle. Another explanation without demonstration followed.

Next up was the plastic head off a Donald Duck Pez dispenser. His students really struggled to comprehend eating something that was made almost entirely of sugar that only had adverse nutritional benefits and they thought he was simply bizarre when he depicted Disney World and all its wonders. His Donald Duck impression was pretty good but it was wasted on his audience who didn't even know what a duck was, let alone a bad-tempered half-speaking duck that was dressed as a sailor.

A crepe pan then caught his attention and though the crowd listened intently as he discussed and explained what eggs, flour and milk were, along with Shrove Tuesday, squirty cream and syrup, he could tell that they were only politely humouring him and did not care a jot.

A sardine can still with congealed tomato sauce around the edges, a faded Twix wrapper, a pair of crusty underpants, a hole punch and a lump of black plastic followed.

It was then that he gratefully saw what he was looking for but he deliberately ignored it for a while, tediously explaining the next four or five items he encountered.

The Alexas were mesmerised by the spectacles and took turns to wear them once he had pointed it out to them. For the six or so generations previously, no one had experienced bad eyesight having been long since genetically perfected, so it hadn't occurred to anyone that you might wear the things.

Eventually Adam turned to the box of matches that he had seen earlier.

"Matches!" he declared. Man's little fire starter. He opened the box. Three matches remained inside. "Let me demonstrate," he said and quickly removed two matches, concealing one between his fingers. "I will strike this little stick on the box here and make fire."

"No!" commanded an Alexa. "Three firesticks. Very dangerous. Fire forbidden. Knowledge sticks work. Replace immediately."

With an over-elaborated huff and a puff Adam replaced one match and was about to place the box back on the shelf when the Alexa nearest him assertively said,

"Stop. Fire stick missing box." The Alexas were as animated as he has seen them and made such a fuss looking for the missing match. All the while Adam squeezed his right middle and ring fingers together, holding the missing match in place.

"There must have only been two," he lied.

"Three," came the response.

After a lengthy but unsuccessful search, the smiling Alexas delivered some alarming news.

"Immediate destruction. Loss forbidden." The words cut through Adam's heart like a knife. They were going to have to terminate themselves for losing the match.

"Me too?" he asked but he already knew the reply so was instigating plan B.

Adam had earlier inserted a piece of twine down his sleeve in the faint hope that lighting it would act like a firework lighter and would stay lit, long enough to get back to his mini bonfire that he had prepared back at his arbeit station.

There was no way that he was leaving the library to go anywhere other than to the pit while the match was missing so lighting his twine was his only remaining hope. He poked the match out from his fingers and scraped it across the wall. Nothing. He tried again harder but this time the match flipped from his grip and landed on the floor right in front of an Alexa.

With a tremendous theatrical performance Adam looked to the ceiling and then all around, surprised as to where the match had come from. "I think it fell from the roof," he stated, pointing and gesticulating all the while in an attempt to cause distraction.

The Alexas had never encountered lying before and, as unlikely as it seemed, accepted Adam's account to his massive relief.

"Go now," said one near the door.

"Ok," said a reluctant Adam, disappointed with the outcome. "Preppers. You simply can't rely on them. I expected box after box of matches. Flares obviously, dinghies perhaps, but mainly matches. It's all they ever go on about. Keep your matches dry," he mimicked.

"Go now," repeated the Alexa.

"I am, I am. Keep your beautiful hair on," grumbled Adam. His eyes then virtually leapt from his head as he spied a small shiny object at the back of the highest shelf nearest the door.

"Wait," he yelped, loud enough that he braced himself for a shock that didn't come. "I need to show you this. It's very important for education. One last thing, just give me a second."

Adam reached up to the shelf and fumbled around with his hand until he laid a finger on a metal box. He gradually slid it towards the edge of the shelf and dragged until it fell and he caught it in his other hand.

"Bingo!" said an elated Adam who was now holding a silver-plated vintage Harley-Davidson Zippo lighter. For a second he was lost in the actual beauty of the thing. It had hexagons in stripes above and below rows of small squares which also formed stripes and the Harley-Davidson logo wrapped around the edge. "Wow. I'll bet this was worth a few bob even back when I came from," he mused.

The "Go now" command of an Alexa snapped him out of his thoughts and he got back to action.

"I have to tell you about motorbikes. It is desperately important education," fibbed Adam. He showed them the logo and then began to describe motorbikes and riding. He made as much noise as he dare, waved his left arm around as much as he could and distracted the Alexas with as many motorbike impressions as he could muster, all the while flicking the wheel on the lighter hoping it would give a flame.

The searing pain of burning to the palm of his hand told him he had been successful. 'Fire forbidden' rang through his head. He had been in this place long enough to know that doing anything forbidden here meant some sort of pain so he held his breath so he didn't scream and shimmied the lighter flame away from his searing skin.

He could smell the lighter fluid and knew that his time before discovery was short. He wiggled the twine from his arm and held it in the flame behind his back. He couldn't see but the plume of smoke that bellowed into the room made him think that it was lit.

The smoke alerted the Alexas whose smiling blank expressions did not take away from their obvious response to danger.

Having never experienced any such toxins, they immediately began coughing, choking and staring at Adam for answers.

He produced the lighter, whose flame was still burning strong. "Fire!" he exclaimed. "Don't worry I will save you and get rid of it."

Adam threw the lighter to the floor right in front of the Alexas who simultaneously jumped away to safety. The cap snapped shut and extinguished the flame. "I saved you all," declared Adam in triumph as smoke billowed from his arm. "Come on. We've got to get out of here. Er, ahem, smoke will probably follow me for a while because I have been near the fire. Don't worry, that is normal. We will all be ok. You probably need to stay well away from me for the foreseeable. I will return to the growing field where I can be safely isolated."

The Alexas, knowing no different bought into his nonsense and left him to his own devices as he galloped to his cabbato field. On arrival, he shooed away field workers so he was alone. He whipped out the twine which was still smouldering and giving off lots of smoke. It barely glowed so he blew on it despite the already oxygen-lush environment. The air movement caused a glow and then another and, after a short but silent prayer to God, a small flame sprang from the end.

In jubilation he set alight his already prepared mini fire and in minutes a small fire heated his fermented liquid. He put the makeshift still together and waited. Low and behold, as the brew heated, a perfectly clear liquid dripped from the end of the copper pipework into his second container.

Adam danced in celebration like he'd never danced before and when he had gathered as much alcohol as he dared without boiling the liquid and ruining it, he very sadly extinguished his fire.

So much effort and this must surely be a one-time project. Adam figured he had about the equivalent of a small beer bottle of booze. He carefully raised his container and took a sip.

The liquid burned through his throat and immediately cut the oxygen from his brain for a second, making his eyes and nose pour in a giant snort. "Bugger me!" he part spluttered, part choked as a rasp of electricity about finished him off. He fell to the floor but somehow held onto his booze container without spilling a drop. Lying on the floor he took another sip and then another. He was very quickly wasted. Operation distillery had been a success.

Adam had the most fun. He drunkenly and unashamedly danced. He laughed like a madman for no reason. He sang beautifully tuneless dirges. He remembered happy occasions and funny incidents but then became overly emotional and cried. Eventually he crashed out face down on the floor wearing half a cabbato on his head as a hat with a moustache drawn across his top lip.

*

The next morning he was seriously hungover. His head hammered like he was being hammered in the head with a hammer. His mouth was a dry as the Sahara and his tongue seemed to be stuck to the back of his teeth. His stomach was bloated and he was passing gas that was so bad it was making him bork with the smell.

A loose hue of smoke still lingered enough to keep him alone but he figured the Alexas would surface soon. He groaned as he hid the remainder of his booze under a pile of rudimentary gardening tools. His liquor had knocked him senseless in only a few sips. He would be a millionaire if he could get this stuff home somehow. The thought of home made him even more depressed than his alcohol heebie-jeebies were making him. What he would have given for a 'Maccie D' breakfast.

Amazingly a fun bar shifted his hangover instantly and he felt as fresh as a daisy. He couldn't believe the transformation. Suddenly bright and breezy he dreamed of making millions of pounds with his three sips drunk, one bite sober products. It wouldn't even take a decent marketing campaign to sell the two as a pair in the normal world. If only he could reproduce them on his return he would be on a complete winner. That was if he could ever get home. That thought brought him down a peg or two. He was facing a lifetime of arbeit in the weird world instead.

Adam decided that he would restrict himself to one booze session a week and that way he would have something to look forward to in his life of purgatory. Catching his reflection in the back of his tools he realised he needed to clean off his drawn-on moustache. In doing so he noticed he was perfectly clean shaven. His hair was cropped short too. His nails were manicured and nice. He hadn't appreciated this before but thinking about it, he had remained this way since day one here. He was aware he had half a beard in the war and had probably arrived at this place in a pretty hairy condition after his jungle trek.

He had previously realised his teeth had never needed cleaning because he never ate anything that wasn't pure goodness although after his drinking party his mouth had tasted like he was chewing a cow's backside. His fun bar had dramatically improved the situation and he hoped a few more might finish the job, but it was forbidden to have more than four a day and only then at set times, so he would have to suffer his donkey breath for a little longer.

He dug his fire ash into the ground, leaving no trace of it and worked hard throughout the day in his field. When an Alexa approached he immediately asked them about his hair and nails.

"Hormone injection. Growth energy wasteful," came the reply.

'Good God,' thought Adam, terrified that he was being injected without even knowing about it. 'I have got to get away from this place sooner rather than later.'

Twenty-two hours from that thought, he couldn't have been more right.

Chapter 18

Death

As boring a day as any followed Adam's drunken antics and he was left to his eleven-hour floor slumber after arbeit. On returning to work the next day, he yawned and stretched and braced himself for another day of tedium.

He was wrong.

As he walked into his field, he immediately saw the slumped figures of two Alexas at the furthest point. They were sitting back to back with their legs out in front of them, feet collapsed to the side. Alexas didn't sit so Adam was immediately concerned that something was amiss.

He walk-jogged towards them, frantically praying that this clear anomaly was nothing to do with him but before he got to within ten feet he could clearly see his booze container sitting at the side of them.

The realisation that he was probably in a lot of trouble was fighting in his mind against how funny seeing two drunken emotionless future clones might be, but the former won when he noticed the colour of the first Alexa he saw.

It was blue. Dark, veiny blue with pink blotches. The sight stopped Adam in his tracks and he drew his hands across his mouth and nose in horror. He slowly walked around the pair and though Adam wasn't an undertaker, medical professional or taxidermist, he knew immediately that the pair were dead. As dead as a doornail as the saying goes.

The electrocution that followed the loud profanity Adam hollered was the least of his worries and he barely flinched at it.

Adam racked his brain for where 'how to hide the dead bodies of two drunken clones' was stored but once again his only knowledge of such things was based solely on his movie experiences. *Shallow Grave* – chop into pieces and bury. *Small Apartments* – strap to a chair, shoot in the head twice and torch. *Weekend at Bernie's* – walk around and pretend not dead.

"Crap," said Adam realising he was screwed, then "Aaaargh! Not now" as quietly as he could manage to the electrocuting suit. Jumping up and down on the spot and spinning around seemed to be his only brain idea and he was seriously starting to panic when he realised the least he could do was hide the now-empty booze container away from the bodies.

He bent down to pick it up and slightly caught his knee on the arm of dead Alexa number one as he did so. This caused the body to wobble. Adam stood palms open to the body. "Steady," he somewhat pleaded but to no avail. The body began to fall towards him. He leapt down to steady it by placing his arms on their shoulders and breathed a huge sigh of relief as he prevented the fall.

A noise behind him made him turn. Whilst he still had his hands on the dead body of one of the two Alexas, he saw that standing behind him was a group of twelve of the beings, all smiling beautifully yet so so sinisterly at him.

"Damn!"

Chapter 19

The Pit

Adam couldn't see into the pit. Not because it was too deep or too dark, but because the extreme stench that was emanating from it was so grotesque he was unable to open his eyes through his grimace.

He stood on the edge trying desperately hard not to throw up for the third time in three minutes, or at least dry heave; fun bars did not afford any waste to repel in such stress situations.

For a moment he pondered if he could have done anything differently that wouldn't have ended with him facing agonisingly drowning in rotting clone corpses deep in the depths of Earth. Probably not distilling alcohol may have helped. It was after all not the first time alcohol had gotten him into trouble. Aged fourteen he had been arrested for being drunk and incapable by the local constabulary after swigging a small bottle of cheap scotch in one. Whilst he always remained proud that he had never failed a down-in-one challenge, standing on the precipice of a tunnel to doom, he considered that perhaps it wasn't the epitaph he had been hoping for.

He realised that he hadn't been listening to the committee member who had been wittering on for some time about paragraph this and that. In essence they were saying that two Alexas had found Adam's booze and sampled the product, instantly intoxicating themselves to just beyond paralytic on the good-night-out scale. Their next gulp of his liquor was fatal, given that their bodies were completely unconditioned to toxins and the worst their limited kidneys had previously had to deal with was some 99% pure H_2O.

Being caught red handed hadn't helped his argument that it was nothing to do with him and now that he was being fingered for the deaths of three comrades, given the speedy recollection of the missing 4323 that was no longer being held on file, he was very efficiently condemned to destruction by pit.

The talking stopped and Adam looked around at the grinning Alexas all gorgeously willing him to drop to his demise. Adam always thought that given the choice of kneeling and being shot to the back of the head, he would have always opted for the 'dive on the assassin and try and bite his face off' approach, regardless of the consequences. He had never expected that he would have to test his courage to do this but here he was with no alternative but to die or try.

Adam squinted and held his breath, long enough to survey his surroundings. They were in a tunnel but it was not painted like the others, instead it had a claggy clay look to the walls. It was still brightly lit with the lighting strips so he could see the opening to the pit which was about fifteen feet wide in diameter and sat clean in the middle of the tunnel. It was a wonder no one fell into it, given the awkward location. There was no safety fencing or flashing warning lights. Adam supposed the nose-splitting reek would be enough to stop a wandering soul from accidentally plummeting to their doom. There were between ten and fifteen Alexas, he couldn't see them all for each other but he did feel they were somewhat eager to see his demise, considering they were supposed to be unfeeling sorts. He heaved one more time before wiping the tears from his eyes and the sweat from his hair.

Adam then smiled at the nearest Alexa with the best smile he could muster and they smiled back at him with that meaningless beautiful smile to which Adam had become so accustomed.

Then he twatted the Alexa so hard in that smile that their perfect teeth shattered into a thousand pieces and sprayed blood all over the next three bystanders.

He swung for a second punch at the next Alexa but not only were they were already off and briskly walking away, their evolutionary fight or flight reaction reduced to flight only, the electric suit attack completely winded him and dropped him to his knees. Adam recovered and went after an Alexa, sucker punching them straight to the back of the head and causing them to fall forward with a thump onto their delightful face.

The resulting electric shock was more extreme than the last but he was ready for it and braced against it. He ran down corridors and through rooms. Alexas were noticcably extremely scarce, such was their inability to deal with anything other than diplomacy, but any one that accidentally found itself in Adam's path also found itself battered to an inch of its life with no remorse whatsoever. Each electric shock hardened his resolve and the primal scream which accompanied the fifth or sixth shrilled and echoed through the caves and tunnels like nothing heard before.

As he galloped about, he found his way to the door to the outside much faster than on his last journey. Adam was exhausted, burnt from the electricity and animalistically hostile towards anything in his path to freedom.

An electronic keypad for the door and two Alexas stood between Adam and freedom. He snarled. They beautifully, yet menacingly, smiled.

Adam growled and a wave of pain shot through him from his suit making him roar a chilling noise from the depths of his lungs.

One Alexa looked at the other who nodded. He braced himself for the fight. Instead they tapped some buttons and the door to the airlock swung open.

Chapter 20

Outside Again

Adam burst into the daylight in pain and in relief. The Alexas did not follow but just in case he bore left and secreted himself under a bush where he could view the outer door and watch for anything untoward.

Secreted under the shrubbery among the leaves and the grasses, he commenced guard duties. His attempt at guard was useless though and instead he very quickly fell asleep. The fear and adrenaline and excitement, and probably the remains of his hangover, knocked him out for hours and when he awoke it was dusk.

With the remainder of the daylight he sharpened two large sticks into spears using a chunk of rock. There was no way he wasn't going to be prepared for any rabid dogs this time. He spent the night under his bush with no massive problems, having eaten and enjoyed the plentiful fruits that were about. A massive insect bite on his leg that instantly turned into a gloopy green blister was his only issue, and though it snagged on his boots and burst quickly, draining goo down the side, compared to his electrocution pain, he barely noticed. He did wonder how he hadn't seen any monster insect take a chomp of him though.

At sunrise he set off on his next journey. He was going home. He didn't know how but he was determined and far more prepared for the challenge, now that he was dressed, booted and armed.

He decided the best course of action was to head to the location he had arrived at on day one. Whilst this seemed like a good idea, finding his way through the jungle remained frustratingly difficult with treacherous natural dangers, unpassable routes and more killer creatures than he could literally shake his stick at.

He had lost track of how many days he had been walking and was sporting a somewhat lengthy beard by the time he gleefully looked out from Hampstead Heath towards St Paul's.

By now he had snagged and ripped his suit in a number of places and had fully lost one sleeve resulting in him having one suntanned arm. He had also found a large metal spike which meant he could successfully hunt. Disappointingly, he couldn't make fire despite hours of stick twisting and blowing so he ate his catches raw, the consequence of which was a blood red hue to his beard. The raw meat eating was at first disgusting yet still he persisted despite the abundance of beautiful fresh fruit everywhere. He didn't know why but he simply craved meat. He enjoyed the thrill of the catch and was cleverly sewing the furry skins together using the metal wire from his suit sleeve which had annoyingly dangled down his arm where his suit ripped, in preparation for this perfectly warm place suddenly turning to a bleak winter on him. Deep down he thought he might be doing it just to piss Darren off. Even in a vegan paradise, Adam wouldn't play ball.

Looking like a cross between Robinson Crusoe and Mork from Ork, he finally arrived at a patch of lush grass that looked more like the patch of grass he arrived naked on than any other he had seen. A few moments earlier he had watched from high up a tree as a huge dog had wandered by, sniffing at the ground where Adam had been standing seconds earlier. As frightened as he was, the dog reassured Adam that he was nearing the right location and he was relieved when it wandered off into the forest disinterested.

Adam now stood on the patch of grass and looked

about at the surrounding paradise. There were no time zones, windows, weird hazes in the air or anything. There was absolutely nothing unusual or different.

Except for a six foot five elderly Alexa dressed in a white, eagle-studded, flared jumpsuit and groovy shades.

Chapter 21

The King

Adam laughed. Belly laughed. Fell-to-the-floor-in-hysterics laughed.

Alexa Elvis smiled pleasantly but was clearly not expecting this reaction from the human so they attempted to repair the situation by doing a full-scale hip-swivelling air-punching Elvis dance move.

The dancing just about finished off Adam, who snotted across his cheek and was struggling for breath at the hilarity.

Alexa Elvis simply therefore stood and smiled while the human recovered his composure.

Eventually wiping the tears away, Adam apologised among little chuckles and introduced himself.

Alexa Elvis introduced themselves as John Lennon which caused Adam to splurt a giant guffaw and crease up laughing again.

When he eventually recovered, he apologised for his rudeness. "I'm so sorry. I've had a terribly hard long journey to get here and you caught me by surprise, John." Saying John made Adam snort a laugh again but he quickly pulled himself together. "Sorry," he added.

"Thank you. Thank you very much," replied John.

Adam fell into fits of laughter again and much of the following day followed the same routine as Adam was introduced to a number of elderly Alexas who were all dressed in differing 1970s bejewelled jumpsuit Elvis costumes with quaffed hair, named Roy Orbison, Hendrix, Bing Crosby, Oasis and Ringo. Meeting Showaddywaddy was particularly hilarious.

The Elvises prepared a monumental meal of cooked

meat and root vegetables and sang and danced as Adam ate it, unable to partake in the feast themselves. They shared the characteristics of the Alexas and yet were at least thirty years older and, although remaining emotionless, were just so much more fun.

After food, all was explained to Adam.

Thirty years earlier a group of Alexas had approached the committee to outline their belief that the direction of life taken was fundamentally wrong and that there was much more to living than arbeit and two year pit destruction.

The group had studied human history and were fascinated by the religion followed by Elvis and millions of people prior to the war of destruction. They discovered that great costumes were adorned by Elvis's followers and had themselves created similar costumes but had been forbidden to wear them by the committee. They discovered that Elvis had twelve disciples named Roy Orbison, Oasis, Showaddywaddy, Bing Crosby, John Lennon, Hendrix, Ringo, Macca, Shergar, Chandler Bing, Maradona and Clint Eastwood.

Each of the disciples was a great entertainer and spread the message of Elvis who was known as the King of rest and recreation. Elvis encouraged the people to relax, work less, live life and dance and sing and this was the fundamental reason for human existence.

The committee were horrified about these discoveries but such were the numbers of Elvis believers they were unable to enforce any sort of pit punishment. Instead, an agreement was made that anyone who wanted to leave could clone themselves, and then do so.

Three hundred Elvis believers each adopted a disciple name and left the safety of the tunnels for the outside world. The committee believed them to have died instantly in the poisonous air. In actual fact most of them died by other means although rather quickly given their complete unpreparedness for survival and their ill-thought-out plan of leaving without fun bars to eat. This led to the excruciatingly painful death of many who needed to excrete waste from their enforced fruit consumption but didn't have the anatomy to do so. An upside-down gravitational method of throwing up had been developed to save the day, although Adam felt the visual demonstration by Oasis was entirely unnecessary and disgusting.

Within the first fourteen months only seven of the Elvis believers remained alive. These, Adam had all met. They had learned to adapt to the hostile world like Adam quickly did. They built a safe home. They developed energy and safe-to-eat bars that caused no excess waste. They made clothes and sang songs. Above all they lived and grew old together.

Twenty-five years later, with aching bodies and failing eye sight, the Elvis believers realised that they needed to do something to protect the future of the human race and avoid the hideous existence that had befallen the Alexas.

It was decided to build a time machine and rescue Elvis Presley from the past. The five-year-long project resulted in a time window being made to enter the last exact location Elvis had been known to occupy.

Adam asked, "How is it at all possible to make a time window?" and instantly regretted it because some very technical and hugely boring physics was then explained to him in monotone for the next few hours and by the end he was none the wiser.

Some ancient film had been located which Adam now realised was from the movie *Pollyanna*. The Elvis believers believed that Elvis liked to marry children so transmitted the footage to entice Elvis into the time window. Something had gone wrong and Adam had entered the window.

Arriving in their world, the Elvis believers were shocked to find naked, scared and confused Adam on the grass rather than the King of R and R in all his glory. They had ducked behind the forest to consider what to do, only for Adam to flee in the opposite direction. A search party had continued to try and locate him but in failure, the decision had been made to ignore Adam's presence in their time and reattempt to bring the King to the future.

Twenty-two more attempts had been made from differing times and locations. None were Elvis. None had reacted particularly well to having been dragged naked into the future. They were interviewed for education and then returned to their world.

"You can return me to my world?" asked Adam with sudden excitement.

"Yes, ma'am, uhuha," replied Showaddywaddy with a hip shake which caused Adam to laugh.

It was explained that a simple reversal of the procedure would return Adam to his world. Adam signed up instantly. He could not wait to get back to… war and death and the destruction of the planet as he knew it. Suddenly deflated he explained the situation to the Elvis believers.

They probed him for more information and, like with the previous Alexas, Adam spent an age explaining everything he possibly could. He carefully worded his explanation of Elvis and his 'disciples', sensitive to completely ridiculing these people's belief structure although he could not resist pointing out that Shergar was actually a horse. The believers did not believe him about that at all. They didn't know what a horse was and Adam's neighing and galloping possibly didn't help create a visualisation of the animal to any decent degree and his argument of "If I'd had some coconuts, you would have known exactly what I was describing" was probably incorrect.

"Why not stop destruction?" said John Lennon suddenly, cutting Adam off mid-flow in his account of Maradona's handball goal at the 1986 World Cup.

"Well yes," said Adam whilst still standing with his fist raised above his head in mid-motion. "How?"

"Block the atomic reaction blah blah blah blah blah," said John Lennon who didn't say blah but it was what Adam heard.

The others agreed. A plan was made. Adam was to return home, wait for the first bomb and deploy some sort of scrambling device that would prevent any nuclear explosions taking place. He had absolutely no idea what anyone was talking about but if it meant saving the world then he was up for it.

The first problem was how to get the device to the past given the time window's ability to completely remove even the traveller's clothing.

Adam would have to learn how to make the device and construct it when he got home. Day one of lessons saw Adam suspended from class for messing around. Day eighty-seven saw Adam stand in front of the Elvises and word-perfectly regurgitate the lesson that had been delivered exactly the same since day one. At least that is what Adam thought happened. In actual fact he got approximately eighty percent of his account entirely wrong.

"I'm sorry. This is some really complicated stuff," apologised Adam, secretly knowing that they were yet to move beyond year 9 dual science levels.

John Lennon had an idea to resolve the matter.

The resulting massive mathematical tattoo all across Adam's body explaining how to make the device hurt more than he ever could have thought possible but seemed worth it in order to save the human race.

The second problem occurred to Adam. "If I stop the bomb, the human race will continue as was and you lot won't exist."

"Understand," said Ringo.

It appeared that the believers were entirely on board with ceasing to exist. They believed they were soon to die anyway and were entirely unemotional about that prospect. They fully believed the ways of the Alexas had developed against all the principals of human life. Elvis taught that singing, dancing and fun was the way of life and not arbeit. They were determined for a better future but changing the past was the only way to get one.

On the day the tattoo stopped glowing red and blistered, and with hugs and best wishes from Adam, which entirely perplexed the believers, he moved into position to be transported back to the past. "Thank you. Thank you very much. Adam has left the building," he said.

Chapter 22

Home

The pain and disorientation to his body was once again awful but Adam quickly found himself lying in a busy London street, naked and freezing half to death.

He stood and rubbed his eyes before being immediately slammed to the floor by a burly police officer who flipped him onto his front, wrenched his arm behind him in the air and knelt on his back.

"Put your other hand in the small of your back," screamed the officer.

Adam obliged and was quickly and effectively handcuffed, before being dragged to his feet and paraded past hundreds of outraged onlookers in all his glory.

A twenty-something punk with facial piercings shouted "Nice tats, man" from across the street. Adam hoped the bloke wasn't Scottish but worried about his physique all the same and wished his hands weren't tied behind him so he could at least try and hide some of his shame.

He knew to keep quiet. This copper clearly wasn't in the mood for chit-chat. He would allow his solicitor to do the necessary with regards to the bomb instructions so he said not a word.

Eleven hours of freezing cold cell confinement with only an itchy and somewhat soiled-looking blanket as a companion followed, but he soon found himself in a plainly decorated consultation room with chairs, a desk bolted to the floor and a poster advising him how to seek treatment for drug misuse. He was adorned in a thin paper suit with press studs for buttons, two of which had completely ripped out of the paper when he tried to snap them shut, leaving parts gaping open. Giles Young, solicitor, was sitting opposite him, frantically making notes in an old leather-backed journal. Giles was in his mid-to-late fifties with a splash of grey hair around a bald and shiny head. He was wearing a beautiful Gieves and Hawkes pin-striped suit. He was experienced and wise and had seen it all before. Adam's lengthy and at times hilarious tale of futuristic Elvis beings was a difficult listen. When eventually Adam finished he carefully said, "Ok, Adam. I think the first point of call is to get you medically assessed and then I suspect we'll be able to get you out of here very quickly."

"Oh I'm fine," retorted Adam. "A few cuts and bruises here and there but that's it." Adam witnessed the uncomfortable look on Giles' face and it dawned on him what the solicitor had meant.

"Oh you think…" said Adam, alarmed, before shouting, "*Twelve Monkeys*!"

"What?" asked Giles.

"*Twelve Monkeys*."

"There were twelve monkeys that you forgot to tell me about?"

"No," laughed Adam. "The movie *Twelve Monkeys*. This is like the movie. The time traveller comes across as crazy and ends up in a mental institute. Aha. I have to avoid the twelve monkeys."

Strangely enough, shouting "*Twelve Monkeys*" did not convince Giles of Adam's sanity in any way shape or form.

*

Four hours later, after telling the doctor absolutely nothing about anything other than that he had been drunk and decided to get naked, a police interview followed where he said the same. Adam soon walked out of the police station in his paper suit and a pair of black plimsolls with a charge sheet for indecent exposure and a date at the Magistrates Court.

He pondered his next move. He needed a scientist who would believe him that the end of the world was nigh and that time travel was possible. This was surely an impossibility.

It turned out it was really easy.

He had returned home, showered, shaved and donned some tattoo-covering clothes. He gratefully found his mobile telephone and wallet on the bedside cabinet and nodded in approval as he found a large wad of cash inside.

When they returned home, Adam showered Darren and Annabelle with love and kisses that were most unwelcome and irritating to them. He said nothing of what had occurred but he cried tears of joy as he hugged Darren with all his strength and he kissed him repeatedly on the top of his head. Annabelle received much the same and he sobbed and sobbed as he cuddled them whilst they tried to wriggle free in disgust at his antics.

The sloppy hugs were followed by over-the-top eating where he wolfed down a can of corned beef like it was a chateaubriand and then ate entire jars of pickled onions and maraschino cherries. When he tried to kiss Annabelle after licking out a Marmite jar, causing her to yelp and scream obscenities at him, his antics certainly roused some suspicions of a mental breakdown in the youngsters.

His twenty-two minute speech on how much he had missed a cup of Yorkshire tea almost caused them to consider calling for help and when Adam insisted they take a month holiday to an isolated pacific island entirely at his expense, the jig was up.

"What's going on with you?" asked Darren. "You're acting deranged. And what's happened to your hair? You look like you're wearing a wig."

"Ah! *Twelve Monkeys*," said Adam.

This didn't help matters at all and as Darren began to call someone, Adam left as fast as he could before men in white coats arrived.

From the park he used his mobile telephone to type 'Anyone know of a scientist studying time travel with a nuclear background?' into Facebook.

Eleven minutes later he had sixteen witty comments, eight links to conspiracy theorists, four absolute nut jobs who he was alarmingly friends with spouting everything from anti-semitism to racial hatred and a direct message from Professor Al Marsh of Teesside University inviting him to a meeting.

Though he had no idea where in the country Teesside University was he immediately agreed and, after a quick google, set off to the North to save the world.

Chapter 23

Professor Marsh

When in a rush to save the world, catching the Megabus north was probably not the best idea. Seven hours and five minutes later, he crawled into Middlesbrough bus station. It was a dark and hostile place, with zombie-like people shuffling through the corridors with no sense of purpose or direction. For a moment Adam wondered if he had transported to a new world again, particularly when he exited through the southern door into a square of deserted closed shops where he was promptly approached by a girl wearing a dress that revealed her buttocks and breasts quite plainly. "Fancy a nice time, mate?" she gruffed through a mouthful of brown stumps.

Her breath smelled bad enough to make him gag and he couldn't even muster more of a reply than pointing and mumbling, "University."

Fortunately, the University and surrounding area was most definitely the highlight of the town and Adam met with the Professor in a modern techy building with more glass than real walls and snazzy lighting that made the whole place look space aged.

The Professor was a delightful man. Adam had expected an old fellow with crazy white hair, a tweed jacket and a monocle, but Professor Marsh was a young guy in his late thirties. He was dressed in distressed Levi's 501s with a too-big silver-studded belt hung from his slim waist like a lasso. He had dirty white Converse high tops and was wearing a green shirt over a white vest. His hair was scruffy and black, as was his stubble, and yet he talked like the imagined monocled professor might in the Queen's best English and with extraordinarily long words. Professor Marsh listened intently to Adam's lengthy story whilst supplying him with copious amounts of perfectly brewed tea and Jaffa Cakes.

Exhausted and trembling, Adam collapsed into his chair when he finished. The Professor nodded and asked one question only.

"Want a Fat Hippo?"

Chomping through a most wondrous burger combination which included chorizo, bacon, Swiss cheese and onion rings, having made the half-hour journey to the beautiful historic city of Durham was enough to double convince Adam that the future needed altering immediately. The Professor was definitely in agreement.

He had barely spoken and, when he did, he grimly sprayed some wonderfully named Fat Hippo sauce across the table prompting both an apology and a delay in conversation.

Meal completion saw the Professor excitedly spring to life. He asked Adam a billion questions which mostly started with "In the future how..?" and mostly ended with Adam saying "Dunno". He made notes from Adam's tattoos and though he lamented that the Elvises had not provided him with details on how to time travel, the ability to neutralise nuclear weapons was hugely satisfying for him. Time and again he said "Haha obvious" as he explained things to Adam which were not in the slightest bit obvious or even delivered in what Adam considered to be real words.

The bit he did understand was when Professor Marsh said "I can have this done by Friday" which was awesome because, by Adam's calculations, that was when the whole world order would break down in chaos and war.

The Professor sent him home and assured him he

would send the device in the mail to him. Given the 'saving the world' element and the ability of Royal Mail to deliver your parcel to a depot fifteen miles away even though you were home the whole time, Adam thought this was the worst idea ever and at first protested. The Professor ushered away his concerns and Adam found himself on the overnight Megabus back to London, worried but satisfied that he had done his bit for humanity.

Halfway home he received a Facebook message informing him that Professor Marsh would activate the device at the appropriate time rather than unnecessarily send it to Adam, which, while it was obviously a good idea, it slightly concerned Adam that he was no longer the man in control.

Chapter 24

Two

In the early morning sunshine, Adam wearily walked home. He had managed to sleep quite well on the bus but all in all events had taken their toll on him and he crashed through the front door exhausted.

Standing in the hallway was himself.

Now Adam had seen all three *Back to the Future* movies and was well aware from the teachings of Doc Brown that coming into contact with yourself in such circumstances had catastrophic consequences. For the life of him, he couldn't remember what those catastrophic circumstances were, but he reacted quickly and belted back out of the door as quickly as he could before running and diving head first into a nearby bush.

The other Adam reopened the door and quizzically looked around before returning inside.

Adam suddenly had a memory of this incident from the perspective of the other Adam and chuckled that his former belief that it had been a postman was quite ridiculous. In full Marty Mcfly style he now had a task not to interfere with the future until the time was right to interfere with the future.

Suddenly he started to panic. If the other Adam lived up to the nuclear war and then Professor Marsh stopped the war, then that Adam wouldn't fight a war, time travel and would live happily ever after. This Adam, himself, now would have to live a life in hiding, watching his former self from afar. This was no good. No good at all.

After deliberating his options, all of which spelled disaster for his own self's future, he decided to contact Professor Marsh and discuss it with him.

"Oh don't worry, my boy," said Professor Marsh in his reassuring and delightful manner, "you'll just cease to exist."

Despite the best efforts of the Professor to try and make Adam feel that this was entirely fine and good, Adam couldn't help but feel like he was being eliminated and an imposter was about to take over his life.

"It's me," he kept telling himself but it didn't make him feel any better and neither did his bank cards and phone being frozen when the other Adam reported them lost.

A sad and gloomy Adam lived in the streets like a homeless person with no money and only Macdonald's Wi-Fi as a lifeline to his former world. He'd changed the passwords to Facebook and Instagram but figured it was only a matter of time before the other Adam sorted that issue out and he lost access.

He spent most of his time watching Darren from afar. Darren was a beautiful boy. Adam watched as he helped an old lady pick up groceries from a split bag. He saw Darren sit with a homeless person and talk to them for twenty minutes. The boy smiled and brought happiness to people. He cared for the planet, joining a community litter event picking other people's rubbish from the floor and he even fed sugar to an ailing bumble bee. Adam was exceptionally proud that his son was a loving, kind human being.

He also watched himself. It was irresistibly difficult not to, despite the unsettling nature of it. Adam found that he picked his nose in public an alarming amount of times and swore to rectify this forever. He thought that he walked like a gorilla and swore to stand up straighter and swing his arms more. He saw himself attempt to put a Double Decker wrapper in the bin, miss and watch it blow away without retrieving it. Poor Darren would probably be picking that up later so he went and retrieved it on behalf of his other self and placed it properly in the bin.

To begin with Adam had watched the girl next door but he had felt like a peeping tom stalker so knocked it on the head quite quickly, although the lasting memory of seeing her drop a robe and walk beautifully naked past the window was serving as a pleasant distraction to his overworked brain from time to time.

Sitting in McDonalds, whilst eating a hamburger and lamenting that he couldn't afford a slice of rubbery cheese for moisture with the money he had painfully scoured from the edges of the street, Adam flicked through the internet. His mobile phone was low on battery and he winced at the prospect of having to beg and borrow someone's charger again. He knew he was beginning to smell and felt like he was pushing his luck at using the swimming baths showers every other day, so he needed to try somewhere he didn't know. He hated that idea because his whole system was to walk about confidently so as not arouse suspicion and wandering about asking directions to the changing rooms was surely going to blow his cover. Perhaps he would give the baths one last go but he always ran the risk of running into his former self and the catastrophic consequences of that. Whilst he was deep in thought about cheese burgers and stinking like a wet dog, his thumb scrolled across the BBC news app.

His eye caught a headline as it scrolled past and he stopped thumbing and took notice. 'Chelsea flower show pronoun offence' filled the screen with a picture of some fancy flower that Adam didn't recognise. He did recognise the foreheads of Ant and Dec that were immediately below, half cut off the screen, which tempted him to investigate what the Geordie duo were up to. Instead he scrolled up frustrated that his ageing eyesight meant his phone was on super-large text so only one story fit at a time.

Manchester United were on a seventeen game winning streak and likely to return to the Premier League.

The biblical site of Eden had allegedly been discovered.

Russia, the Koreas and China had signed a military pact with the Taliban and multiple African dictatorships severely heightening the chances of an immediate European invasion.

Professor Alan Marsh of Teesside University was claiming to have developed technology to end all war.

"Waaah!" yelped Adam, causing a kid with snot candles mixing into ketchup above his top lip to point and laugh, before his very agitated mother stopped shouting at the child who was screaming for a balloon and directed her vitriol at Snotty with a whack across his head.

Adam read with enthusiasm.

'Gay Teesside physics professor saves the world. A University researcher claims to have developed technology that will end all war. Professor Alan Marsh who has been at Teesside University for twelve years published a paper yesterday which has caused more than a modicum of interest from academics, governments and the military alike. Marsh claims that he has the technology that will neutralise the nuclear reaction in weapons and plans to demonstrate his methods on Wednesday morning. "Nuclear war will be impossible forever," stated Marsh. Government officials were not so ambitious. A source in the ministry for defence said, "We have not had the time to properly consider these claims but it is very unlikely that this is possible. We await Wednesday's results with interest." The BBC's correspondent for Science and Technology, Susan Hemingway, said, "The level of mathematic complexity shown by Marsh's document is of a level never seen before and it remains to be seen whether it is correct. Needless to say, scholars from around the world will be frantically working on this to test the accuracy and content. We watch this space with interest." The Pentagon failed to comment but Twitter users have condemned the news. "Poppycock," said one tweet which generally summed up the Twitter feeling. @Soldierboy, however, was more animated, tweeting, "If nukes are out then we are back to hand to hand street fights. Bring it on." The BBC will be present at Marsh's demonstration.'

'Trump Blames Nun for Sex Romp' was immediately above in the headlines list and Adam laughed that saving the world from nuclear weapons hadn't made the lead story. He looked at the time on his phone, 11.59. It was Wednesday. He wondered how the gay professor was getting on.

"Gay," said Adam out loud. How the hell did that have any part to play in the story? Darren did have a point half the time. The media was ridiculous and this was the BBC. He smiled and shook his head then tried to scream in severe pain but he couldn't make the sound.

Chapter 25

Failure

Adam thought he was dead. First, an unbearable pain wracked his body to such a degree that he screamed through his veins and pores.

Then he was hot. Not painful hot but 'been on holiday to Turkey and sunburnt' hot.

'Pain. Heat,' thought Adam. 'Crap. I'm in hell.'

He always knew that kissing Veronica Chalmsworth on a drunken work night out one year into his engagement to his wife was going to come back and haunt him and here it was. Hell. It seemed harsh, he thought, but other than deliberately popping Tim Line's football as a kid he couldn't think of anything else he had done wrong that might warrant an eternity in damnation. And Tim Lines was a bully. A hair-pulling, arm-punching, name-calling bully. He deserved to have his ball popped. Adam was doing his primary school a solid favour.

God's standards of behaviour were horrendously high to have landed him here.

Adam realised he could feel long soft warm grass under his body and he scrunched his back into it and smiled. The heat was relentless but not actually unkind and he slowly realised it was the beautiful warmth of the sunshine that sizzled his skin.

He nervously opened one eye and then shut it tight, fearful of what he might find.

Then he leapt to his feet, wide eyed, and suddenly fully aware of where he was. He looked around as his hearing kicked in. The sound of the waterfall. He knew it. Thick lush grass surrounded by large colourful blooms of red and yellow and pink. The grass forming a small opening in a thick oak woodland. Palm trees. Lemon trees. Banana trees.

"Oh crap."

Adam was back in the grassy area in the future. He looked down at his naked flabby body. There were no tattoos.

He groaned and held his hands to his face, his brain working overtime.

'Dog,' he suddenly thought. 'I better get out of here before I'm chowed by monster mutt.'

"John Lennon," shouted Adam, "Showaddywaddy. Er, Liam Gallagher. Damn it I can't remember their names. Lennon!"

"Uhuh," said John Lennon as he pirouetted from the vegetation with an overstated hip thrust. "Thank you, thank you very much," he said for no apparent reason.

"John Lennon, thank God," said Adam. "We have got to get out of here. A massive rabid dog is about to come out of those bushes just over there."

John Lennon stood in stunned silence, frozen in confusion and bewilderment.

"Come on," yelled an animated Adam before grabbing his hand and dragging him into cover as a giant bluebottle buzzed by.

Still John Lennon failed to speak and they watched as the giant dog surveyed the area, sniffed at the ground where they had recently stood and followed their scent.

Adam could barely breathe and he was grateful that John Lennon looked simply astounded and frozen so was not likely to make a noise.

The dog reached to within twenty feet of their location when a loud crack caused all of them to jump. The dog jumped highest and bolted off to the left and away.

Adam breathed a huge sigh of relief and reassuringly

informed John Lennon that all was well. A noise startled him and he was relieved to see Roy Orbison and Ringo smiling and walking towards them in their full Elvis garb.

Before he could stun them into shock by knowing them, John Lennon got in first.

"Knows us already," said John. "Know how not."

Adam insisted on gathering the others before explaining all.

Once together he told them of his previous trip. Of the plan. The tattoos. Professor Marsh. Nearly bumping into his other self, how proud he was of Darren, and of the naked girl next door.

The naked girl next door actually took up an unequal and somewhat irrelevant amount of the story, so much so that Adam realised this and smiled as he again remembered the moment.

After much deliberation it was explained to Adam that, probably, in getting Professor Marsh to prevent the nuclear wars, the nuclear wars never happened and everyone progressed with their lives in peace and harmony. The Preppers need not have prepped and were not the only surviving humans. The tunnels were never made. Cloning was never established. None of the Elvis supporters actually existed. They didn't invent time travel. Adam didn't come to the future. He wasn't tattooed. He didn't teach Professor Marsh how to eliminate the nuclear threat. The nuclear wars therefore happened. The Preppers survived in their tunnels. Cloning occurred and the Elvis supporters left the tunnels. They invented time travel and Adam has arrived in this place ready to save the world.

"What?" said Adam seven times before Ringo answered and began to repeat what had been said.

"Wait," interrupted Adam as his brain put all the pieces together. "What you're basically saying is that if I change the future by messing with the past, the future doesn't exist so stops me from being able to mess with the past and then I can't change the future and the past remains the past and the future remains the future."

"Affirmative," said Ringo.

"So I can't actually change the future by changing the past?"

"Affirmative."

"Well that's rubbish."

"Affirmative."

"And it's all been a grand waste of time."

"Affirmative."

"Oh sod off with your affirmatives. Why didn't you know this would happen? It's bloody obvious if you think about it."

Adam sat seething as the Elvises explained that they were well aware that changing the future with the past was impossible but having invented time travel, they wanted to bring the King of R and R to the future to lead them.

"You prize knobheads," was as much as Adam could muster.

He sat in angry silence pondering what had occurred. All that he had been through. All the pain and heartache. The effort. The risk. The painful tattoos! Was all just so these self-righteous idiots could have Elvis to themselves. Adam suddenly laughed. "If you'd brought Elvis from the past to the future, he would have... what...? Disappeared into thin air. This would have fundamentally changed everything. He wouldn't have sung 'Glory Hallelujah'. He wouldn't have died taking a crap on the toilet. Pricilla may not have kept Graceland. Haha. Depending when you nabbed him, he might never have worn those crappy 1970s jump suits you so love. The future would have changed and you morons wouldn't even believe in him. What's to say the war would even have occurred? A missing Elvis might have brought about some sort of other cult hero who completely transformed world thinking. You fools are so blinded by religion that you can't see through your own hypocrisy. Divs."

The Elvises looked crestfallen as Adam's words hit home but Adam was in full rant and kept going in his rebuke.

He ranted about them playing God. He called one of their haircuts awful. He moaned that they'd ruined his life. He kyboshed any hope of ever helping them to get Elvis and he pointed a lot and even spat onto Showaddywaddy's foot which he knew was both disgusting and unnecessary but admittedly enforced his point with shocking brilliance.

Then he asked, "How come I can remember? Surely if I've just arrived here from the past, then I haven't yet gone in the tunnels. Met the Alexas. All that. I certainly haven't been tattooed." Adam pointed to his naked torso, suddenly conscious that he was still unclothed.

Hendrix stepped forward from the group. "Not know," he said whilst clearly keeping his feet out of the way should Adam attempt to spit on him.

They explained that the other humans had returned almost immediately and returned to their time without being away. There should be no memory but if the brain worked in a way no one understood and stored any memory of the time-leap then it would surely have felt like a dream or deja vu. Apparently on their meeting with Adam, he had told them his time had been different. He had made significant inroads into the future. If the Elvises found him unpredictable, violent and dangerous and his story of killing Alexas in the tunnels terrified them, Hendrix predicted that they must have decided to send him away with the false hope of changing the future in order that he had purpose and remained friendly to their group. They would have expected that he would return, in the time loop, and nothing would change.

That he popped into their time remembering a future that hadn't happened yet that was his own past was shocking to their core. They hadn't anticipated it at all. It shouldn't be possible because it shouldn't be that Adam that was in the timeline. It should be the other one. The one who had reported his phone, wallet and some of his clothes stolen. The Adam before them should have been erased along with his tattoos.

"Other Adam wouldn't have reported his phone, wallet and some of his clothes stolen because I didn't come back with the tattoos and take the bloody things. Because after I did do that, everything was switched back to normal," yelped Adam through gritted teeth.

"Confusing," said Ringo.

"No shit confusing," yelled Adam. "You tosspots have messed with something that even you don't fully understand and it's come back to bite me right in the arse."

"Heaven theory," said Hendrix with one of those insipid smiles so common of the Alexas.

"Which is?" asked Adam, fearing that some giant mathematical equation was about to form part of the lengthy explanation.

"When space and time end. All timelines come together. Heaven!" Hendrix smiled.

"What, so you're saying that when you interrupted time and space, time and space thought that I'd died and erased the other me and joined us together in heaven but then you couldn't manage to leave me in that paradise and dragged my sorry arse back here to go through all my trauma again?"

"Affirmative," said Hendrix.

"Well, wouldn't there be lots of other versions of me kicking about in loads of different dimensions? Why don't I have their memories? Like if I'd have dared ask Ailsa Wilkinson out when I was fourteen and she'd said yes and was my girlfriend, I would remember that. Or the version of me that didn't turn down being in the Airforce so I could go to the footy. I would remember that. Or the version of me… well you get the bloody idea. Why can't I remember all the stuff from all the other dimensions of me?"

Nobody replied. Adam sat glaring grumpily at a group of grinning Elvis Alexas and he was fuming.

His faith in God and Jesus was being severely tested. If these futuristic weirdos were right, heaven was potentially a gap in time and space where a billion versions of you, from a lifetime of every possible scenario that your life could have taken, joined together as one. Where did that leave God or was that what God had created? To give you all of the experiences you possibly could have had must have been what God wanted. Maybe that was heaven.

Adam snapped from his thoughts and aggressively asked, "Now what happens?"

"Return," said Bing Crosby.

"Return! Return!" exclaimed Adam in an increasingly shrieky voice. "And do what exactly? Hang around with the other two versions of me until the universe can't cope anymore or the bastard Chinese and their many mates drop a nuke on my head?"

The Elvises shuffled uncomfortably saying the odd "Uhuha" between themselves whilst Adam stomped away and munched on a most delicious apple.

As he crunched on the succulent flesh he had an idea, which albeit a pretty ropey solution was the best he could come up with. He sighed whilst he finished his apple and rethought the plan in every which way he could, never coming up with a better alternative.

"Right," he shouted. "I'm going for a wash. You lot get me back home."

Chapter 26

Perfect Timing

"Two hours and seventeen minutes. Not three hours. Not Bulgaria. Not 1878 and definitely not where I'll get meat-axed by an over exuberant copper. You owe me this," directed Adam and, just for good measure to add a decent element of sinisterness to his instructions, "or when I come back, I'll kill you all before you have any idea that I still remember what's been going on."

John Lennon gave a reassuring hip thrust and fist punch with a confident "Yes Ma'am" and began doing whatever it was he did to make time travel happen.

After searing pain and heat, Adam landed half deaf and half blind in the deserted and dusty street of war-torn London town. Everything was damaged in every way and rubbish and rubble was strewn around the ground where destroyed cars sat burnt and black. The British weather was half freezing him to death and his immediate action on recovering his senses was to locate some clothing. He was about to throw some rubble through the intact window of a giant Primark store when he noticed a trendy boutique shop named Changes a few doors down. The window was already entirely through and, though the clothing near the door was covered in broken glass which was troublesome for his bare feet, he crossed unscathed into the remainder of the shop where he casually browsed as though he was shopping for a special occasion. He picked himself a beautiful One Like No Other long-sleeved shirt in powder blue with handstitched lace stripe and flower-print cuff, a pair of Professor Marsh style Levi's 501s in dark wash, Calvin Klein underwear, Paul Smith socks in a flamboyant zebra pattern with zebra motif and a pair of yellow Onitsuka Tiger Mexico 66, like the ones Uma Thurman wore in *Kill Bill*.

"Typical that I look the best I have in ages on the day I officially die," he said to himself in the full-length mirror ahead.

He grabbed a black leather belt and a pristine white handkerchief on his way out. "Sorry," he said to the CCTV camera on the way, "but the world's coming to an end and I needed to be nicely dressed."

He then went back inside and added a really smart Rolex watch to his collection from a stainless steel cabinet which was foolishly unlocked. With two hours to go, he noticed from the timer, he was cutting it fine. He heard the first nearby explosions rattling through the city and crudely smiled.

The worn faces on the British civilians, manning defence positions with their hastily cobbled together weapons and uniforms, were both terrified and perplexed as Adam sauntered past their lines wishing them a good day in his dapper new clothes.

He crossed streets and bridges, picking his way through the debris and very shortly marched straight through his front door with one big breath.

Annabelle was in the hallway, screamed and ran to him hugging his neck and planting huge kisses on his neck and cheeks. Darren heard the commotion and followed suit before pulling off, noticing Adam's dandy outfit and saying, "What the hell? Have you robbed a boutique or something?"

"Yes. I have," said Adam with a giant smile. "I just walked right in and helped myself."

Annabelle's disbelief that Cain's well-to-do father would go a lootin' just because there was a war on almost led to an argument, but Adam was so pleased that normality had resumed even only for a moment, that he smiled and grinned and let her... them... go on at him like a stuck record. He even called them A which worked a charm at shutting them up.

Checking his new Rolex, which prompted a yelp of "You stole a Rolex too", Adam said to the pair: "Right you need to trust me and listen very carefully. As you know I've been to the coal face of this war and it's not going well. In..." He checked his Rolex again, taking a moment to admire its beauty "...just over an hour, those Eastern forces are going to storm through the streets of London and the merry band of architects, baristas and school teachers will only hold them up for the amount of time it takes them to get brutally killed. The result will be all-out nuclear war. I've found somewhere safe where we'll survive this."

"Bollocks," interrupted Darren.

"Your bollocks will be a little dust shadow, sunshine, if you don't shut the hell up and listen to me," growled Adam. "I have it on the best possible authority there is that this is going to happen."

"Who? Who in any authority is speaking to you? What are you, Montgomery's first general now all of a sudden?" rasped a clearly annoyed Annabelle.

"Alexa. I asked Alexa." Adam smiled beautifully in his best impression of the clones. "Then it was confirmed by John Lennon. Satisfied?"

"No!" hissed Annabelle and stormed away.

Adam reasoned with his son with more success. He pleaded the importance of their leaving right now and Darren left to speak to Annabelle to try and win them over.

They returned some ten minutes later after Adam had paced the floor to threadbare carpet levels, praying that this was going to be successful. Each were carrying a large rucksack and an even larger suitcase. Annabelle had a tatty teddy bear under her arm and was wearing a sombrero.

"You're not going on holiday. You need literally nothing," began Adam before realising now was not the time to argue so he grabbed the rucksack from Annabelle and said a cheery, "Well done you two. That was some incredible packing."

They left the house without even closing the front door, Adam rushing the others along as they dallied for keys and suchlike.

"Head that way and wait for me on the corner by the pub," instructed Adam. "I'll be along in a minute." He doubled back and nervously approached the house next door. He tentatively knocked and was overcome with sadness when there was no reply. He knocked louder and when there was still no reply tried the door handle. It was locked. He peered through the window and saw there was no sign of life. He was gutted. Worse than gutted. He felt like he didn't want to go through with his plan after all and would stay and wait until she returned from wherever she was. He hadn't realised how much she meant to him until now. Now that it was too late. He booted the door in anger and frustration.

"I hope you're not intending kicking it down," the girl next door said from behind him with a beautiful grin which was immediately showered with kisses from a delighted Adam.

She somewhat fought him off before shyly saying, "Adam. I'm not that kind of girl. I don't kiss before the first date."

He responded by hugging her so tightly that she could barely breathe. When he eventually let go he mumbled, "I… I…"

"What, Adam?" she replied with a look of both bewilderment and happiness on her face. "Come on now.

Spit it out."

"I think I love you," he said. "I thought I'd lost you. I thought I'd missed my chance."

"Chance at what?" she teased.

"Forever happiness," was his perfect reply.

She barely took any convincing to go with him. Since the recent death of her mother, she was all alone and since the fighting had started she was terrified to stay in her home on her own. She took more convincing that she didn't need any stuff with her so he relented and added to Annabelle's rucksack with two large carryalls and a large picture of a horse which clearly had sentimental value though he didn't have the time or inclination to ask how or why.

They caught up with the others and silently and nervously set off towards the fighting. Darren and Annabelle merely cast Adam impressed winks and smiles but said nothing.

Chapter 27

Together

Annabelle was cross. So was Darren. It wasn't really surprising. For the last thirty minutes or so, they had been shot at, bombed, blasted and were now covered in blood, mud and tears. Worse was that Eileen bear, her prize possession from a time when she was still a girl, was now missing half a head and had splinters of someone's teeth stuck to the fur.

"Please just trust me," screamed Adam over the noise.

"I trust you'll get us killed here," snapped Annabelle. "You didn't say anything about getting shot at when you mentioned somewhere safe."

"To be fair you have completely done us there, Dad," said Darren. "It's amazing we're in one piece."

The girl next door was tremendously calm and held Adam's hand, having abandoned her bags minutes into reaching the fighting. "I'm just glad you came back for me," she said.

Adam, though, was preoccupied. He could see Linton and his other self pinned down yards up the road and under fire. Old Bill was laying wounded behind the Renault Clio, alive but not for long.

"When the Clio explodes we need to run and run hard," screamed Adam to the others. "Please, please, please leave your bags. You don't need them where we're going. We have to go down the edge of those buildings then cross the gunfire towards Pollyanna. You might see double. Ignore it. It's... er... normal to have hallucinations in such situations."

"Pollycrappinganna?" spat Annabelle seriously on the brink of losing their mind. "Pollybastardanna? Crossing gunfire? Are you stark raving mad?"

The Clio exploded, drowning out the rest of Annabelle's words and sadly killing Bill once more. Even though he was expecting it, Adam still felt a horrendous pang of sadness but he composed himself quickly and shouted, "Run!"

Holding hands tightly, he set off at a fast run, dragging the girl along who gamely followed. Darren gave chase, turning and waving forward a protesting Annabelle who stood steadfastly for a moment before deciding running was probably better than being blown to pieces where they stood.

The four of them bounded down the building line, dodging shrapnel and dead bodies. Through the smoke Darren saw his father break from the buildings and run flat out across the road under a hail of bullets towards a flickering image of a small girl in a pretty dress and they stopped in their tracks screaming "Daaaaaad" as Adam vanished from sight.

"Don't stop. Keep going," said Adam alongside them. "I know it's confusing but trust me. I love you, son. You need to trust me."

Annabelle joined them and timidly said, "I'm scared. What's going on. I just saw… I just saw… you… you killed." They began crying.

"We've got to cross that road and we've got to do it now," said Adam sternly.

"I can't do it," Annabelle cried. "I'm not going," said Darren.

They huddled together in tears and fear. Adam hugged them both.

"Darren. Annabelle… Cain. A. My children. My heart. My loves," he said softly. "We've got to do this. There's no other option. We'll be safe. Where we're going there's no discrimination. Everyone's equal. You can be anything and anyone you want to be. We cross this road and we'll be happy."

Without a word they looked at Adam, then at each other. They hugged and moved into position to go and didn't hear Adam say under his breath, with a smile, "And I've got a human-race-saving job for you two that you're not going to like one bit."

With a huge sigh of relief Adam then turned to his new love. "You ready to do this?" he asked.

"I'm ready for our life together," she said. "I've been dreaming about it forever."

"'I'm sorry. I don't actually know your name," Adam said embarrassed and with a wince.

"Eve," said Eve.

"Hi, Eve. I'm Adam," said Adam. "I know," she said and kissed him.

*

Captain Linton rubbed his eyes in disbelief as he first saw Adam run across the road before being obliterated out of existence and, thirty seconds later, Adam again. This time nattily dressed like he was at a night at the pub, holding hands with a beautiful woman in a red flowered sundress and followed closely by two handsome youngsters, one of which was carrying a suitcase and half a teddy bear. They flat out ran across the road and disappeared without a trace.

Epilogue

Burbank California,
27th June 1968 A.D.

Scotty Moore, Dominic Joseph Fontana, Charlie Hodge, Alan Fortas and Lance LeGault were all dressed in matching dark red suits and sat huddled on a small stage, somewhat like an open boxing ring, surrounded by a lush red carpet playing their musical instruments. Fontana, the drummer of the band beat an old guitar case with his sticks rather than his usual drums. Among them, a beautiful thirty-three-year-old man, dressed in black leather shirt and trousers played acoustic guitar and sang. He crooned 'That's Alright Mama' with a curled lip, floppy quiff and killer smile.

The audience sat politely around and briefly clapped as they listened to the movie star perform in a way he hadn't for many years. As the song reached its final throes, they clapped along with increasing vigour.

In row C, seat 22, a most incredible looking girl sat a whole head and shoulders taller than everyone else. Despite her beauty there was a peculiarity about her in the way she wore her hair not too dissimilar to the singer and was dressed in a bejewelled jumpsuit not of the contemporary fashion, which she had carefully crafted that day from other garments she had borrowed.

As the song ended, screams from the audience made her body try desperately hard to stand up and flee but she resisted and maintained her distant expression and beautiful smile, politely clapping along. During the training for her mission she had been warned that screaming would occur as humans could not contain themselves.

He was after all the King. The saviour of the future.

About The Author

From the age of 21, Robert J Walker spent his adult life in the fight against crime. It was a life that always delivered the unexpected. Twists and turns along the investigative journey were normal. Unspeakable horror that most people could never even imagine was his day job.

Armed with this wealth of gritty crime experience, Robert wrote a book – an amusing story about relationships, the future and Elvis, without a hint of crime to be found.

With a close, huge, and wonderful family, Robert is lucky to be surrounded by love and encouragement.

He has a passion for football, food, music, the great outdoors, and loves an adventure.

Experiences, new and old lead to story ideas and Robert plans to keep writing. Perhaps he may even write a crime novel or two.

www.blossomspringpublishing.com